AMBER FISHER

SIN & BONES

LIGHTS, CAMERA, MYSTERY
3

intro reel (recap)

Welcome to *Sinful House*, a reality TV show where the 7 Deadly Sins live together in the sunny beach town of Odyssey, California, and compete to become America's Favorite Sin!

Previously on *Sinful House:*

1. Pride learned supernatural bounty hunter Walt Romanowsky believed local actress Charmaine Young might be a selkie—a shapeshifting seal
2. While investigating Chenoweth International, Sloth and Pride recruited Wrath to hack Walt Romanowsky's laptop. They uncovered the organization's website, which included a shopping page for MagicBloc products and a marketplace for the buying and selling of supernaturals.

3. Sloth and Pride went to visit Eleanor
    Romanowsky to tell her what they'd found
    on her son's laptop. When they arrived, they
    found Eleanor murdered and her pet birds
    stolen…
4. …but Eleanor's ghost was still lingering
    around. Pride and Sloth took Eleanor to the
    Crypt, a secret underground location that
    serves as the headquarters for the Odyssey
    Paranormal Research Society.
5. Pride discovered an old map of Odyssey
    hidden inside Walt's laptop.

You're all caught up! Stay tuned for more rollicking adventures. And don't forget to vote for your favorite sin at the end of each challenge.

Happy watching!

one

. . .

"**S**weet mother of pearl, what on earth is going on here?"

I had just returned from my morning jog on the beach to find Sloth, Wrath, and Greed milling around in the front yard. It was early, and Sloth should have been asleep. Instead, she was standing barefoot in the grass wearing her ratty bathrobe, a steaming mug of coffee in her hand. When she saw me, she waved me over, tittering.

"Isn't it amazing, Pride?" she asked, her voice thick with awe. "I mean, can you believe it? We haven't even been here a whole season, and already the Star of the Sea has paid us a visit."

My eyes traveled to the enormous mermaid statue that had appeared in our yard. It had to be at least 20 feet tall. It hadn't been there yesterday. Heck, it hadn't been there when I'd left for my jog earlier that morning. "What's it doing here?" I asked.

"Bringing bad luck," Sloth answered matter-offactly. "At least, that's Greed's theory. That's why he and Wrath are trying to dig her up. If you ask me, it won't work."

I clucked my teeth. "Why not?"

Sloth leaned her head to the side and said sleepily, "All of us are right where we belong. Even the Star of the Sea. Our task is not to find fertile ground upon which to grow, but to learn to bloom where we are planted."

I scoffed. It was way too early to argue over cliched aphorisms (even if that particular saying was one of the most cockamamie things I'd ever heard) so instead I said, "I shouldn't be surprised by anything that happens in this town. And yet, I keep being surprised."

"That's a good thing," Sloth said. "When the world stops surprising you, it's probably because you're dead."

I wrinkled my nose and peeked inside Sloth's coffee mug. It didn't *look* like she'd spiked it with anything, but she sure was talking like she'd had one too many down at Sailor's Drink and Sink. Still, she wasn't entirely wrong.

Since coming to Odyssey, I'd seen a lot of weird stuff. I'd seen a woman turn into a nine-tailed fox, a dead man trapped in a psychic's body, and an army of wights working as servers in a Chinese restaurant. Mostly, I could explain these things. Well, not scientifically. But at least they jibed with my experiences. I could accept that shapeshifters existed. After all, I'm a psychic who talks to ghosts and has visions when I touch people. So I could accept that a dead man might get trapped inside another person's body. I could grasp how undead spirits consigned to an eternity of servitude might get roped into working food service. Death is unpredictable, is what I mean. So is life, for that matter.

But statues? Statues are usually predictable. And that's why, even after everything I'd seen, I was surprised to find the city's mascot looming over our yard.

"Last week, she was standing on the roof at JB's Groceries," Sloth said. She was watching Greed and Wrath alternate between pulling and pushing the statue to no avail. "Apparently, she was holding a bag of cash in one hand and an AK-47 in the other."

I chuckled. "Are those rifles even legal in California?"

"They are if you're a statue," Sloth answered, not missing a beat. "She's *supposed* to carry a lantern and a mirror. Her right hand lights the path ahead while the left reflects on the past. She's supposed to stand in front of City Hall to remind visitors of what is possible and how far the city has come."

I nodded. "Portia Cameron told me the statue disappeared from in front of City Hall a while ago. She's been traveling all over town. Nobody knows what to make of it."

"I tried asking her," Sloth said.

"Asking who? Portia?"

"No." Sloth sighed. "The Star of the Sea. I tried asking her what she hopes to accomplish by roaming the city."

I did a double take, but Sloth's expression was serene. She looked serious. "Are you for real?"

Sloth shrugged. "You never know if you don't try,

right? She wasn't sharing her secrets with me, but maybe Wrath and Greed will have better luck." She giggled as she took a sip of her coffee.

Across the yard, Greed and Wrath were doing…something…to the statue. Wrath was wielding a shovel, trying with little success to dig up the earth around the mermaid. He looked hilarious—he was wearing skate shoes and black parachute pants with a white nylon pullover. The guy had obviously never done an honest day's work in his life, and it showed.

Digging my hands into my pockets, I ambled over to where Wrath had dug the shovel into the ground. He was bouncing on the step of the blade, trying to use his body weight for leverage. It wasn't working very well. "Morning," I said. "What's going on?"

Wrath didn't look up but gestured with a tilt of his head toward the statue. "What's it look like? The stupid statue's in the front yard! We have to get it out. This is a sign, man! She's not supposed to be here."

I rubbed the nape of my neck warily. "No, she's not supposed to be here. But why is it a sign?"

Greed used his hand as a visor as he peered up at the statue, an angry scowl scribbled over his face. "I had a premonition," he said.

Now, that piqued my interest. In the time I'd known Greed, I hadn't seen him do anything particularly psychic. To be fair, I mostly avoided him. He creeped me out. He gave off distinct vampire vibes with his aloofness and pale skin and long, dark hair. Not that I believed in vampires. But I still didn't want to spend time with people who looked like they might take a bite out of my neck, given the right opportunity.

Still, I *was* curious why the two least athletic people in the house were digging up the mermaid. "You had a premonition? About what?"

Greed's gaze drifted toward me, his expression icy. "An unexpected visitor will bring disaster and bad luck," he recited. He jammed his thumb in the direction of the wandering statue. "She's an unexpected visitor. Unexpected and *unwanted*. So I've recruited Wrath to help get rid of her."

I frowned. "Your premonition sounds like a bad fortune cookie," I mused. "Do they always sound like that?"

Greed returned his gaze to the statue. "Do you always *smell* like that?"

I took a step back, an embarrassed flush climbing up my neck. I'd just returned from a run on the beach. I wasn't supposed to smell like roses, but I guess I was a little ripe. "Well, that was rude," I muttered. "Anyway, Wrath seems to be the only one working. Are you going to help him dig?"

Greed folded his arms across his chest. "We're taking turns," he informed me. He said this like it was the most obvious thing in the world. "I sent Gluttony to the hardware store to get another shovel. Although our house is well-appointed, I guess no one expected us to do any actual yardwork. The garage and toolshed are both wanting. Since we only have the one shovel, only one person can dig at a time."

Well, that made sense. "Okay. I have another question. How do you know the unexpected guest is the statue? That seems like a stretch to me."

"Does it?" Greed's eyes narrowed, his lip curling in a flash of anger. "On the same morning I had the premonition, the statue appeared in our front yard. Doesn't feel like a stretch to me. In fact, I'm annoyed my premonition is lagging. Usually, I get at least a few days' notice before something happens."

I hrmmed noncommittally. "Right, okay. But how is getting rid of the statue supposed to change our future? The unexpected guest has already appeared, right? Does digging her out prevent the disaster or whatever?"

Greed stepped toward me, his expression changed. He no longer looked angry. Now, he was looking at me like I was stupid. I think I preferred it when he was angry. "You don't read tarot cards or anything like that perchance, do you, Pride?"

I scoffed. "Of course not. I may be a psychic, but I don't buy into that cockamamie nonsense."

Greed stretched his lips in a vampiric facsimile of a smile. "Cockamamie nonsense. I see. You do have a way of stating your position on things, don't you? No matter. If you did read tarot cards or perform similar work, you would know that no one's fortune is ever set in stone. All we can do is predict the most likely outcome based on a person's current situation and trajectory. For example, if a student continues not to study, he's likely to fail the test. If an employee continues to do mediocre work, he is not likely to get promoted, and may even lose his job. And if you continue to let an unwanted guest stand guard over your house, something terrible is likely to happen."

I frowned, scratching my chin. "The first two examples I get, even though the second is not necessarily true."

Greed snorted. "Isn't it? Mediocrity is seldom rewarded."

I shrugged. "Well, you've clearly never worked in corporate America. Anyway, even if your first two examples are sound, I'm not sure about the last. No, don't bother explaining it to me," I said, holding up a hand to stave off his interruption. "My interest in this topic is very low."

I turned my attention to the offending statue, really taking her in for the first time. She was beautiful. Cast in bronze with a white marble base, she was a wonder. I could see how she must have been a welcoming fixture in front of City Hall with her lantern and mirror. But now, both her hands were empty. Her palms were pressed to the sides of her face, the fingers curled inward. Her eyes were wide and round, and her mouth was open wide, her jaw stretched. She was screaming. The statue looked terrified.

My stomach flipped over. I didn't believe in omens as a rule, but when I got a load of her face, the strength of my belief system took a nosedive. There was something deeply unsettling about her, and the more I looked at her, the more I felt something twisted and dark settling into my bones.

I looked away.

"Have you reported this?" I asked. "To the mayor or whoever?"

Greed grunted. "What good would it do? Do you think the city will send someone to dig the statue out? Because if you do, please say so. I would gladly hand the manual labor over to someone else."

"You already did," Wrath grunted, still trying to overturn the soil. He chucked the shovel to the ground and propped his hands on his hips, leaning his head back in exhaustion. "I hate to admit it, but Pride might be right. We've been digging all morning, and the statue hasn't budged. Maybe we should call someone."

Just then, a car pulled into the driveway. Gluttony emerged from the driver's side and hauled a shovel from the backseat. He slammed the car door shut and stalked over to Greed, thrusting the shovel into his hand. "You owe me $20," he grumbled. "You can pay me later." Gluttony turned to me, his eyes flitting to the statue. "What do you think of her?"

A breeze blew, ruffling my hair, but it wasn't the warm, salt-scented breeze from the Pacific Ocean. It felt more like an electrical disturbance, an invisible current that passed right through me. I shuddered against the sudden cold, and my skin pimpled over.

Gluttony must have noticed because he looked me up and down and frowned. "Are you all right?"

I nodded, stammering. "Fine. It's just…there's something about that statue. Seeing her up close like this… she gives me the willies. I don't like her."

Gluttony grunted. "I guess nobody does. Me, I don't believe in bad luck, but y'all can think what you want.

Greed and Wrath are out here busting their rumps because they think this here statue is bringing some bad juju. But me? I think she just wanted to be on TV." He lifted his chin toward the house.

I turned, following Gluttony's gaze. Sure enough, the camera crew had gotten wind of our new guest and was assembling on the porch, filming the whole thing. Wrath made a rude gesture at them. That would get cut in editing.

Greed tossed the new shovel to Wrath before retrieving the other from the grass. He attacked the topsoil with a vengeance. "I won't take this affront lying down," Greed said tersely. "If I have to dig all day, I will. But I'm not one to merely sidestep challenges fate has left in my path. I like to obliterate them. That's how I operate. That's how I've gotten this far in life."

"Well, good luck with that," I said, turning toward the house. "I guess I'll see you all at dinner?"

Wrath looked up, his brow creased. "Hold up, you're not gonna help dig? I've been at this all morning."

"Can't," I said with fake regret. "Envy and I are going over to the mortuary. We have a case of talking corpses to solve." I rubbed my hands together in mock anticipation and let the statue-inspired gloom roll off me. "Anyway, I hope the two of you get the statue out of here sooner rather than later. She doesn't look like she wants to be here any more than you want her here."

While Wrath grumbled something else that would get cut in editing, I disappeared into the house.

"If I were a dead person, I would absolutely want to be buried here. This is the kind of place I'm destined to sleep the eternal sleep in." Envy peered through the passenger's side window, her face pressed to the glass. "I didn't even think they had places like this in California. It looks like something you'd find in a Southern Gothic movie."

As I drove slowly down the driveway, I had to agree with her. If we hadn't just turned off Ocean View Drive, I'd never have believed we were still near the beach. I mean, the place had magnolias and weeping willows, for crying out loud.

Though, to be fair, we were pushing the boundaries of Odyssey. Remembrance Home was on the other side of town from Sinful House, tucked away in this idyllic glade.

"Place looks haunted if you ask me," the camera guy said.

My old camera guy had left the set for unknown reasons, and I had a new guy. This one was built like a refrigerator, with shoulders like boulders and biceps the size of a baby's head. He was wedged uncomfortably into the back seat, his knees practically pulled to his chest. I wondered why the network gave us such small cars if they were going to hire such big camera guys.

"Thankfully, no one asked you," I said absently. "Now zip it. You know the saying. It's better to be silent and be thought a fool, yadda yadda."

Beefy Camera Guy blinked in surprise but said nothing more as he turned to look out the window.

As we pulled through the long driveway, I slowed my

pace to get a look at the building. Unlike most of the architecture in Odyssey, which was a cross between Spanish and beachy chic, Remembrance Home was one of those traditional colonial-style buildings. A broad porch wrapped around the weathered brick building. It even had plantation-style columns. In iron letters across the front were the words, REMEMBRANCE HOME. It looked exactly the way you would expect a funeral home to look. Polished, but not overstated. Elegant without being standoffish. And only mildly haunted.

We weren't going directly to the mortuary, however. The family who ran the place, the Thorntons, had an attached home on the east side of the building. As we walked up to the front porch, Envy placed a hand on my arm, giving it a gentle squeeze.

I paused to look at her. "Something wrong?"

Envy's eyes widened, and she shook her head, her face cracking into a smile. "No! Nothing's wrong. I just wanted to say I'm really excited to be working with you on this case."

"Oh." I hesitated, waiting for her to say something more. When she didn't, I gestured toward the door. "Okay if I ring the bell?"

She nodded enthusiastically. "Go ahead. I'm ready to get this party started."

I rang the doorbell.

A middle-aged woman opened the door. Her hair was a mousy brown and hung straight just past her shoulders. She wore a floral dress, nude stockings, and a polished pair of white flats. She looked nothing like the other women I'd met in Odyssey. She looked more like a preacher's wife in middle America. Not that I'm an expert. "You must be Pride and Envy," she said.

"That's us," Envy chirped. "I'm Envy. That's Pride. And that's the camera guy, but we don't know his name. So!" Her smiled widened. "We're here to see someone about corpses waking up in the middle of the night."

The woman smiled and extended a hand, which Envy and I both shook. "I'm Danielle Martin," she said. "Please, come in. Let's get acquainted in the living room."

We followed Danielle into the house. She led us into the kitchen where a breakfast table was set with lemonade and cookies. The three of us sat down, and Envy grabbed a snickerdoodle.

"I really appreciate your coming," Danielle said. "Before we get down to it, I thought I might explain what's been happening and why we asked RealTV to help. The whole thing has me a little flustered."

Envy chuckled. "I would get flustered, too, if I were embalming a corpse and it suddenly started talking," she said. "But don't let me get ahead of things."

"Well," Danielle said, "I wasn't the one embalming. My father, Edgar, is the mortician. He doesn't know I've asked you here to investigate this. Oh, I guess I should begin at the beginning."

Envy jabbed a finger into the air. "And when you come to the end, stop."

Danielle nodded. "It all started a few weeks ago. My family has been caring for Odyssey's dead for genera-tions. My grandfather started the business. When my father passes on, my brother and I will inherit it.

Anyway, Daddy was embalming Fiona Arquette when this whole thing started. Daddy was already in a bad place because he and Fiona were best friends, and he took her passing hard. In high school, everybody assumed they'd get married. That's how close they were."

"Were they sweethearts?" Envy asked. "I'm a sucker for a high school sweetheart story."

Danielle laughed. "No, never. From what I hear, Fiona was always sweet on Julian Gillespie. The three of them were like Gene Kelly, Donald O'Connor, and Debbie Reynolds in *Singing in the Rain*. Though between us girls, Julian has nothing on Daddy. Daddy is a genius, and Julian is a blockhead." She paused, shaking her head. "Oh, I shouldn't say that. He's the mayor now. Don't put that on the show," she rushed to add, blushing furiously. To Envy, she said, "He won't put that on the show, right?"

"Who, the camera guy?" Envy smirked. "He doesn't edit the content. He just shoots it. So, go on with your story. The mayor's an idiot, and your dad is the Smarty McSmartyPants of their friend group."

Danielle squirmed, shooting nervous glances at the camera. "Well, I don't know if I'd say the mayor's an *idiot*," she hedged, twining the pearl necklace at her throat around a slender finger. "He's just not the brightest bulb. I remember when he first ran for office, he was worried he wasn't electable because he didn't grow up rich. Odyssey is like that, you know. Very big on appearances."

"So we've noticed," I said.

"Right. Well, Julian badly wanted to win. So he asked Fiona if she would join his opposition's campaign and spy for them. Fiona, bless her heart, was willing to do it. But Daddy had to gently explain to both of them that no one would fall for that. Their friendship wasn't exactly a secret."

Envy laughed politely. "Sounds like your father has a good head on his shoulders."

"Oh, he does," Danielle gushed. "He does. But I do think losing his best friend has skewed his judgment. Not that I can blame him for that. Everybody loved Fiona, and I mean everyone. She was a performer and the life of any gathering. All the moms wanted her for their kids' birthday parties. She had these puppets, and she'd read these terrific kids' books, and she'd do all the voices and everything." A cloud passed over Danielle's face. "I hadn't seen her in years, though. Not since she developed the Alzheimer's."

As much as I didn't want to be rude, none of this was relevant to our case, and my interest in this woman's life story was very low. "Maybe we should get back to the talking corpses."

Danielle collected herself and nodded. "Yes, of course, sorry. I do go on sometimes, don't I? My husband always says if talking were an Olympic sport, I'd be sure to come home with the medal." She tittered and waved her hand airily. "Okay, sorry! Anyway, Daddy was working later than usual that night. I didn't think much of it because he's always been a night owl. I figured he was working slow because Fiona was a friend. The next day, he told us what happened. Just after 3 a.m., Fiona Arquette started talking."

Envy leaned forward. "What did she say?"

Danielle grimaced, wringing her fingers in her lap. "Well, I wasn't there, but Daddy said it was gobbledygook. It was all stuff like, 'Infrastructure costs are rising. Natalie agreed to lead next month's bake sale.'"

"That is strange," Envy said. "Who's Natalie?"

Danielle shrugged. "Who knows? Probably no one."

"Interesting," I said. "And was that the only time this happened?"

Danielle shook her head. "Not at all. Cougar Whitecastle and Jody Helmuth were the following night. And just like Fiona, they spoke gibberish. After that, Daddy got smart and recorded the incidents on his phone. I'll get you those recordings, though I have to tell you, they're confusing."

"Did the deceased have anything in common?" I asked.

"Nothing I can think of," Danielle said. "Just that they lived in town."

"How many talking corpses were there in total?" Envy asked.

Danielle thought for a moment. "Well, let's see," she said. "Fiona, Cougar, and Jody were first. Then there was Freddie McIntyre, Inez Montoya, Jack Wilcox—that was crazy because Jack shouted his message—and...oh, yes. Monica Stewart. I think that was everyone. So that's seven."

Envy glanced over at me. "Do you think that's significant? Seven corpses? Seven Deadly Sins?"

I grinned and shook my head. "Not everything is about us, Envy." To Danielle, I said, "So why did you ask the network for our help? Aren't there locals who dabble in this kind of thing?"

I was thinking specifically about the Paranormal Research Society operating underneath the coffee shop Déjà Brew, but I was pretty sure they were a secret, so I didn't ask directly. Danielle twisted her hands in her lap. "Well, that's the sticky wicket. See, Daddy doesn't want me or my brother involved in this at all."

"He doesn't? Why not?" Envy asked.

Danielle sighed. "He says he has it all under control. He says I don't need to worry about it—he's already handled it. A very Daddy thing to say, honestly," she added with a soft smile. "But it's not helpful. This is a family business. And like I said, one day, it will be half mine. If I'm inheriting a haunted mortuary, I think I deserve to know about it. And if it's *not* haunted and something else is going on here, I think I deserve to know that, too."

Envy nodded sagely. "Yes, you certainly do." She glanced at me and raised an eyebrow. "Pride, do you have more questions?"

"No," I answered.

"Well, in that case, unless there's more you want to tell us, do you think we can meet your dad? I've never met an actual mortician before."

Danielle brightened and got to her feet. Envy and I followed suit. "Well, sure! I'll take you back. Honestly, I thought he'd be in by now. Even for him, it's getting pretty late." She glanced at the clock. It was just after 9 a.m. I guessed he preferred to work at night. "Just do me a favor and don't mention anything we talked about, okay?"

Envy made a motion like she was zipping her lips and throwing away the key. We followed Danielle outside and down a little pathway that led to a side entrance. We padded down a wood-paneled hallway that led to a set of stairs going down.

At the bottom of the stairwell, we passed through a door marked *EMPLOYEES ONLY,* and the ambiance changed. Instead of rich carpet, the floors were tiled. Wood-paneled walls were traded for unadorned white drywall. Danielle pushed open a door marked *PREPARATION ROOM* and stepped inside. "Daddy, are you still working? It's already morning! I've brought someone who wants to meet…"

Her words fell away as she screamed. I hurried into the room, pushing Danielle aside. When I saw what caused her reaction, I stopped short, my throat tightening. Images of the screaming statue filled my mind, and my heart sank into my shoes. The bad luck Greed promised was apparently already starting.

Lying in the middle of the floor was a man's body.

He'd been shot in the chest.

He was dead.

two

. . .

"**D**addy!"

Danielle rushed toward the corpse, falling to her knees at his side. Tenderly, she rolled him over and pressed her fingertips to his cardioid artery. It was obvious her father was dead, even to me, and I'm not exactly what you would call a professional. His skin had taken on an ashy pallor, and his limbs were stiff. He looked like he'd been dead for at least a few hours. Danielle pulled her hand away, choking with sobs. Then she grabbed him by the front of his protective garments, pressing her forehead to his chest. "Daddy, please wake up! Please wake up, Daddy!"

I pulled Envy aside and said, "I think you should probably call the cops."

While Envy dialed, I moved to Danielle's side, placing my hand gingerly on her shoulder. "There's nothing you can do for him now," I said, pulling her away from the body. "Come on. You shouldn't be looking at this. Let's get you somewhere else until the police arrive."

But Danielle didn't budge. "Who could do such a thing? My father was the kindest, gentlest man anyone ever knew. Why would anyone murder him in cold blood like this? It just doesn't make sense. It doesn't make sense!"

I knew these questions were rhetorical, so I didn't answer them. Instead, I helped her to her feet and led her out of the room and back up the stairs. I didn't know the layout of the funeral home, so I had no particular destination in mind. I ended up dragging her along with me until I found a quiet corner for us to sit in. She collapsed into an armchair, her palm pressed to her forehead as tears streamed down her face. "What am I gonna tell Mama? I can't believe this is happening."

A moment later, I heard footsteps coming down the hallway. I looked up to see a man hurrying toward us, his expression troubled. He was very good looking, with a head of thick, dark hair and a strong jaw. He ignored me completely as he made a beeline for Danielle. When she saw him, she jumped to her feet and threw her arms around his neck, her sobs redoubling.

The man pulled Danielle close. "Dani? What's wrong? What happened? I heard screaming! Are you hurt?"

As Danielle continued to sob, the man's gaze slowly drifted to me, his eyes full of questions and accusations. I held my hands up, palms out, shirking off responsibility. "It's not my place to say," I began, "but we found something disturbing downstairs."

"It's Daddy," Danielle said, her words thick with grief. "Daddy's dead, Tony. We found him dead in the preparation room."

"What?" The man's body stiffened, and he drew Danielle away from him by her shoulders to look her in the face. "Daddy's dead? Are you sure? What happened?"

Danielle shook her head as her wailing continued. "He was shot! Somebody shot Daddy!"

"Envy's calling the police," I said. "They're on their way."

Tony glared at me again. "And who are you? What are you doing here?"

"I'm Pride," I answered. "Who are you?"

"Tony Thornton, Danielle's brother." He glanced down at his sister. "Have I lost my mind, or did this person just refer to themselves as *Pride?*"

I opened my mouth to respond, but Danielle beat me to it. "Tony, this is one of the psychics the TV show sent over."

Tony stiffened, his skin blanching. "Oh, Danielle. You didn't."

"He wouldn't let me help!" Danielle sobbed. "I needed to understand what's happening to our *business!*"

"Dani, you invited reality show parasites to Remembrance Home? These people aren't professionals; they're *actors!*"

"Common misconception," I said, "but not true. In my previous life, I was a paranormal investigator." Tony was still staring daggers in my direction, so I plundered on. "We might be able to help. Ideally, I'd like to interview the man who..."

As soon as I said the words, an idea struck me. The last time I'd encountered a dead body was at Mrs. Romanowsky's house. Amid the chaos, I had almost failed to notice that her ghost lingered behind.

I wouldn't make that same mistake twice.

"Excuse me," I said.

Before Tony could ask where I thought I was going, I made my way back to the preparation room. The room wasn't very large and had no good place for a ghost to hide. Still, some spirits were more obvious than others. Some looked like fully fleshed-out humans, while others were merely a glimmer of light. I didn't see any fully fleshed-out humans, so I waited patiently for something to catch my peripheral vision.

But I didn't see anything. For better or worse, Edgar Thornton's ghost wasn't in the room.

I heard motion behind me and turned to see Envy coming into the room. She walked over to me, but her eyes were on Edgar lying stiff on the floor. "Who could do something like this?" she whispered.

I scoffed. "In *this* town? I'm starting to think treachery and murder are just casual pastimes. Ever since we've been here, terrible things keep happening."

Envy shuddered. "You're right. Which makes you wonder. Did the network choose this location because terrible things often happen here, or are terrible things happening because we are here?"

It was a good question, but one that had no answer, so I let it go. Plus, I didn't like to get philosophical this early in the morning. It set a rotten mood for the rest of my day. Not that my day was off to a great start.

"Let's go upstairs," I said. "This is a crime scene now. The longer we stay, the more likely we are to mess something up."

Envy cast a sidelong glance at the door. "I don't know, Pride. Don't you think we should investigate?"

I frowned. "Why would we investigate? You called the cops, didn't you?"

"Sure, but our task was to find out about the talking corpses. Once the police get here, everything will be out of our hands. If we're going to find any answers here, we need to look now. For starters, we need this phone." Envy strode over to where Edgar's phone lay on an embalming table and quickly stuck it in her pocket.

I gave Envy a dubious look. "You know you're tampering with evidence right now, don't you?"

But Envy waved this away. "Forget that. We need the phone more than the police do. And we need to do one more thing, Pride."

I already didn't like the sound of that, but I asked anyway. "What thing?"

Envy gulped. "I think you should touch him," she whispered. "Isn't that a thing you can do? Touch corpses and have visions or whatever? We should know as much as we can about his death. Touch him, Pride. Let's see what he saw in his final moments."

I didn't think it was a good idea for lots of reasons, but Envy was right. If we wanted to win our challenge, data would give us a leg up. Cautiously, I maneuvered myself next to the corpse. I shot Envy one last hesitant glance before I closed my eyes and placed the flat of my palms against Mr. Thornton's cheeks.

I waited, my breath held in my throat. But after several seconds, I shook my hands and stood up.

"Nothing," I said. "I didn't see anything."

"How is that possible?" Envy asked, incredulous. "Don't you always see something when you touch a corpse?"

I looked back down at the man lying dead on the floor. There was nothing unusual about him other than the hole in his chest. But she was right. It *was* unusual for me to touch a dead body and not see anything at all.

"Try one more time," Envy said. "Come on, Pride. Not guts, no glory."

With a sigh, I pushed up my sleeves and grit my teeth, ready to lay my hands once more on the corpse when a gruff voice called out, "Stop right there. Hands where I can see 'em, pal."

I froze, my hands lifted in midair as I turned around. The cops had arrived and were now filing into the room, each of them throwing Envy and me dirty looks. I'd seen these particular cops before. They'd been on the scene when Walt Romanowsky was found dead in the walk-in freezer at Wights and Wongs.

One of them came over to me, notebook in hand. "You the two that found the body?" he asked. His nametag read "Farley."

"Can I put my arms down?" I asked.

Officer Farley glared at me. "If you promise not to touch any *evidence*," he said, glancing down at the man on the floor. "That's what you were about to do, wasn't it?"

"Yes, but it's not what it looks like," I mumbled, lowering my arms to my sides.

The cop scoffed. "I bet." He lifted his chin to the embalming table across the room. "Who's on the table?"

Without waiting for answer, Officer Farley sauntered over to the embalming table and took a quick peek. Then he stepped back, giving a low whistle. "Well, what do you know? Looks like Karen McMurtry finally bit it."

"You know her?" I asked.

"Of course I know her," he sneered. "You can't live in Odyssey without having at least one story about Karen McMurtry ruining your life." He gave the corpse another contemptuous look. I swear, if we hadn't been standing right there, he might have spit on her. "Not so high and mighty are you now, huh, Karen? Your life-wrecking days are over!"

"Can I just mention really fast that you're being extremely rude to a dead woman?" Envy interjected. "I mean, what the heck?"

Another officer, a woman, sauntered over to us, thumbs hooked in her belt loops. "Karen McMurtry had a reputation as a gossip," she explained. "And she was…I don't know, what's the adult version of a tattle-tale? Karen liked to tell people's business—especially business she wasn't supposed to know about, if you know what I mean."

I didn't know what she meant, but I wasn't about to admit that. "Was she a psychic?"

The second cop, whose nametag read "Underwood," snorted. "No, she was a busybody. She liked to say she was protecting the town from wickedness, but really, she was just raking the mud. Couple months back, she found out two members of the city council were having an affair. She told Stephanie Jones about it, of course. Those two were thick as thieves. Stephanie posted about the affair in her community newsletter. It was a huge scandal."

That piqued my curiosity, but also turned my stomach. I'd had my own run-in with Stephanie Jones, and it wasn't pretty. She'd spotted Envy and me at the grocery store wrangling an earth elemental that had gone haywire. Trouble was, she thought the elemental was a little person and published a furious write-up about the incident in her "newsletter"—which was little more than a thinly veiled gossip rag. She'd painted us as "ableist tyrants," an epitaph Envy took particularly hard. The network received dozens of complaints, and Envy lost some Instagram followers over it. It was an ongoing problem.

"So how did Karen die?" I asked. "Was it suspicious?"

Officer Underwood shrugged. "Don't know. Didn't work the case if it was. But if you ask me, if somebody did her in, they did this town a favor."

"Well, I didn't ask you *that*," I said, frowning.

Envy elbowed me in the side and turned an apologetic smile to the officer. "Did Karen ever do anything to ruin *your* life?"

The officer paused, her lips pressed into a line. Finally, she said, "Not unless you count stealing my boyfriend in high school. But maybe that was actually a favor. Sterling Longfellow was Mr. Popular back when we were kids—quarterback, prom king, you know the type. But I guess you could say he peaked in high school. These days, he's just a sorry slob, getting hammered over at Sailor's Drink and Sink with the other losers before noon. He doesn't even have a job. What a worthless—"

"Got it, thanks," I interrupted. The last thing I had time for was some pathetic story about the high school stud washing out as an adult. Why some people stay stuck in high school nostalgia is beyond me. "Are we still needed, or can we get out of here?"

Officer Underwood shrugged. "Do what you like. Just make sure you don't leave Odyssey. Farley and I might have more questions later."

As we headed upstairs, Envy asked, "Can you imagine Karen McMurtry stealing Officer Underwood's boyfriend?"

I stammered, blinking back my confusion. "What are you talking about?"

"Well, I know she's dead, so she doesn't look her best," Envy said, "but did you *see* that woman? She wasn't exactly Hottie McHottiePants if you know what I mean. And Officer Underwood? All that long, red hair? What a looker! If I looked like her?" Envy sighed wistfully. "Well, I wouldn't be wasting my time interviewing psychics in a mortuary, that's for sure. I'd be staking out all the gyms in town looking for a hot guy to buy me drinks and wife me up, you know? I'd put even the likes of Lust to shame."

I filed that away as information to forget later. "Anyway, let's see if Danielle knows the passcode to her dad's phone. Otherwise, your evidence tampering will have been for nothing."

Envy nodded, completely oblivious to the reproach in my voice. "I was thinking the same thing. She's pretty emotional right now, though. Should we try the brother?"

I sighed. "We can try. I don't think he likes me much."

Envy patted me on the arm. "You're an acquired taste. Let's let him have another lick."

I filed that visual as something to forget immediately.

———

Back upstairs, we found Danielle and Tony in a large sitting room. A cluster of cops was off to one side, speaking in low voices. No one bothered the grieving family. But as soon as we entered the room, Tony Thornton's expression darkened, and he climbed to his feet, striding over to us.

"You're still here?" Grabbing us by our arms, he hauled us aside, out of his sister's earshot. "I assure you, your services are no longer needed. Talking corpses are the last thing my sister needs to worry about."

I folded my arms across my chest and lowered my voice. "I don't mean to be a jerk," I said, "but we're investigating this one way or the other. If something strange is happening in Odyssey, we have an obligation as a community to look into it. Don't you think so?"

Tony faltered, for a moment looking unsure of himself. But the expression was fleeting. He straightened his spine and adjusted the tie at his throat. "You're not even really part of this community," he hissed. "You're actors on a reality TV show. Show some respect. Let my family grieve in peace."

I was preparing another statement about grieving through action—some cockamamie nonsense I must have picked up from Dr. Xena— when Danielle joined her brother at his side. She placed a hand on his arm, giving it a little squeeze. "It's okay, Tony. I'm stronger than you think. And I want to know what's happening here."

"Dani, Dad said he was handling it! He didn't seem that upset. Maybe you should let it go."

Danielle sniffed and shook her head. "I want answers. I *deserve* them."

Tony grunted and threw me and Envy a dark look. "I need some fresh air." He didn't look back as he stormed out of the room.

Danielle watched her brother leave and then turned on an apologetic smile. "Please forgive my brother," she said. "He means well, but all of this makes him very uncomfortable."

"Psychics? Talking corpses?" I asked. "Or reality TV?"

Danielle hesitated. "It's not that he doesn't believe in psychics and fringe science and things like that. He does. Maybe too much. He's one of those people who thinks these things are…well, I don't want to say sacred, but not fit for public consumption, anyway. He finds your show distasteful. He thinks people with gifts like yours should be searching for a higher truth, not flaunting their abilities for a quick buck."

"How about flaunting our abilities for a roof over our heads?" I muttered. "Even psychics need to eat."

"I know, and I don't share my brother's position. However, Odyssey is a unique town," she continued. "Many strange things happen here. And when you grow up in a place like this, it can make you hungry for answers."

Sheepishly, Envy pulled Edgar's phone from her pocket. "I took this from the preparation room," she said, delicately changing the subject. "This is the phone he recorded on, right?"

Danielle nodded. "Yes, that's right. I suppose you need me to unlock it." She took the phone and tapped in the code. Then she opened the settings and removed the security precaution. "There you are," she said, handing the device back to Envy. "I hope that's helpful. And please, if you find anything, let me know. Don't let my brother dissuade you. Things have been…difficult for him lately."

"And now his father's dead," Envy mused. "I imagine things will only get worse."

Danielle nodded, stroking the back of her neck with her fingertips. "It might be uncouth of me to share this, but financially, things have been strained for Tony. He joined a…well, I don't want to say cult. That's such a loaded word. But these people took him for everything he had. He was different before. Now, he's so angry. Anyway, it damaged his pride, I think. He's always looking for a way to get back on top. Have you ever heard of cryptocurrency?"

I nodded. "Sure. It's like fake money."

Danielle frowned, her shoulders sagging. "I don't know if that's accurate, but I see where you're coming from. He calls it investing. He says it's the way of the future. But to me? It just looks like gambling. He has no reason to believe these 'investments' will pay out over time. I wish he'd just invest in corn futures like everyone else."

"Not a lot of money in corn futures," I pointed out.

"Not a lot of money in crypto either, if the market crashes all the time," Danielle shot back. "He's lost so much already. He and his husband fight all the time. But anyway. Listen to me babbling on when you have more pressing matters to attend to." She shook off the previous conversation and let her breath out in a whoosh. "Now, my brother is right about one thing. I should be with my family. So, if there isn't anything else you need, may I walk you all to your car?"

It was perhaps the politest version of "Please get the heck out of my house" I'd ever heard in my life. I was impressed. Envy, the camera guy, and I followed Danielle out of the house and back out to the street. As we got into the car, Danielle leaned down to speak to us through the window one last time. "You can call me any time," she said. "My number's in Daddy's phone."

Once we were on the road back to Sinful House, Envy turned in her seat, angling her body to face me. "Okay. So what do you think so far? Did any of your psychic senses go off or anything?"

I shook my head, keeping my eyes on the road. "No, nothing. The place isn't haunted, that's for sure," I said, directing this comment to the cameraman in the back, who only grunted in response.

Envy sighed thoughtfully, running her fingers through her hair. "It's strange that you didn't see anything when you touched Mr. Thornton's body. Something about that funeral home just isn't right."

"Speaking of things not being quite right," I said, "what was that back there? Danielle just started telling us her brother's financial problems. I mean, I know she's talkative, but that was weird, right? Seemed like a very private thing to tell strangers."

Now, Envy made an irritated sound in her throat and rolled her eyes dramatically. "Oh, *that*. That was nothing. I have that effect on people. They don't call me a muse for nothing, you know."

I stole a quick glance at her. "A muse? What are you talking about?"

"That's my gift," Envy explained. "Or, one of them, anyway. I get people to talk. They muse aloud about all kinds of things—everybody becomes an oversharer. Or sometimes I just inspire them. Maybe they know just the right thing to say at just the right time. That's the most common. But sometimes, I give them a perfect idea, and the next thing you know, they're furiously drafting up business plans for an exciting new venture."

"I didn't know that about you," I said. "I thought you just conjured elementals."

Envy sighed. "Well, it's not something I like to talk about. I mean, it's depressing. Do you know how annoying it is that everyone around me is writing the Great American Novel or submitting fabulous new inventions to the trademark office while I'm stuck teaching second graders how to memorize 50 state capitals to the tune of *The Blue Danube?* As gifts go, mine is Stupid McStupidPants."

"So you don't have any great ideas of your own?"

Envy turned to stare mournfully out the window. "Not a single one."

three

. . .

When I got back to Sinful House, I made my way to my favorite location—the kitchen. With any luck, I'd find something tasty in the fridge. And if I was doubly lucky, it would be something tasty with no pesky magic baked in.

Living with a kitchen witch had its pros and cons. On the one hand, the kitchen was usually stocked with delicious meals and scrumptious treats. On the other hand, you never knew what magic might be lurking inside. I still wasn't over the time Gluttony put complimentary magic in the blueberry muffins, and I went around telling everyone how gorgeous their smile was for hours. It was humiliating.

Unfortunately, the kitchen was empty. So I made a sandwich, poured myself a glass of milk, and headed up the stairs. I was halfway to my room when Sloth peeked her head out her door.

"I thought that was you," she said. "Can I talk to you for a second?"

I shrugged. "You're talking to me now."

Sloth giggled like I'd said something funny. "Sure. Well, I just wanted to follow up about Walt's laptop. You did give it to the cops, didn't you?"

My stomach dropped into my shoes. Sloth was talking about the laptop Mrs. Romanowsky gave us before she was murdered. It was now a major clue in the case. I was supposed to turn it over to the police.

Which I hadn't done. But I had a good reason for it.

I wavered. "Yeah, so, about that. We should discuss this in my room."

I led Sloth into my bedroom and closed the door behind us. I gestured for her to take a seat on the bed, even though I wasn't sure I wanted her to do that. I couldn't see any visible signs of spilled food or coffee or juice on her clothing, but that didn't mean there wasn't something hiding. Sloth seemed to have a gift for grime.

"So here's the thing," I said. "See, the laptop…"

Sloth squinted at me. "What about it?"

I huffed out a sigh and strode over to the dresser, where the laptop was hidden under a mound of folded laundry. I swept the clothes aside and handed the computer to Sloth.

She looked down at the jumble of cracked plastic and gasped. "It's completely ruined," she said. When she looked up at me again, her eyes were wide and her mouth gaping. "How did this happen? What did you do?"

"It was an honest accident, I promise," I explained. "There was a sock stuck in the back of my drawer, and I was shaking the dresser trying to get it loose. The computer was on top, and it fell to the floor and shattered."

Sloth stared at the broken heap for a while before setting it aside with a melancholic sigh. "Poor Mrs. Romanowsky. She'll never get any justice now."

"Well, about that." I knelt at the side of my bed and slid my hand underneath the mattress. I found what I was looking for and handed it to Sloth. "When the laptop shattered, I found that inside."

Sloth peered down at the paper she was holding as she began chewing on the end of a pigtail. "What is this?" she asked.

"Obviously, it's a map of Odyssey, but I have no idea what part of town or anything like that."

Sloth flipped the paper over, saw that the back was blank, and then flipped it again. "This looks like a child drew it."

"Yeah. I don't know why it was hidden in the laptop. But I do know somebody really wanted that map. I think that's what they killed Mrs. Romanowsky to find."

Sloth traced her finger along the lines of the drawing, taking it all in. Not that there was much to take in. The whole map looked hastily sketched, and almost nothing was labeled. When her finger found its way to the lower right-hand corner, she paused and read aloud, "Historic Odyssey Nexus of Power, 1902." She looked up at me, her expression thoughtful. "What do you make of it?"

I sat down beside Sloth and examined the map over her shoulder. "Nothing yet. I mean, I don't know. But look at this right here." I tapped the corner of the map with my finger. The map depicted a collection of narrow mounds like skinny hills. Underneath the mounds was a star. "Don't these look like headstones to you? Graves?"

Sloth cocked her head sideways. "I guess so."

I frowned. "If this was a cemetery back in 1902, it must still be here, right? You wouldn't just bulldoze a cemetery and develop it, would you?"

Sloth shrugged. "I mean, it happens. Didn't you ever see that movie *Poltergeist*?"

I hadn't seen it, but I wasn't going to admit that. "What does that have to do with anything?" I asked.

Sloth made bug eyes, looking at me like this was the stupidest question I'd ever asked. "Well, the whole point of the movie was that they built a housing development on top of a sacred Indian burial ground! That's why the houses in the neighborhood were all messed up. Geez, Pride, you really need to get out more."

I didn't say anything to that. I plucked the map from Sloth's fingers and set it aside before she could ruin it. While she was spoiling the plot of *Poltergeist*, I noticed a smear of peanut butter or maybe honey on her hands. "So, what you're saying is, in movies at least, nothing is sacred."

"I'm just saying, I wouldn't rule anything out," Sloth said. "You know, if you want to know more about how Odyssey *used* to be, we should talk to their historical society."

My eyebrows shot up. "There's an Odyssey historical society?"

Sloth shrugged. "Beats me. You didn't even check?

Geez, Pride. That's like the first thing you should have done. Here."

Sloth pulled out her phone and started a Google search. The only relevant entry wasn't for a historical society at all, but for the City Hall. Sloth clicked the link, anyway.

"It says here the official historical society disbanded a few years ago. But it also says that visitors who want to know more about Odyssey's historic roots should direct their inquiries to Mrs. Pamela Arquette."

"Hold on," I said. "Arquette? Really?"

"Yeah." Sloth handed me the phone. "Why, does that mean something to you?"

"Sort of. The task Envy and I are working on involves a woman named Fiona Arquette."

Sloth clapped her hands together in excitement. "Ooh, that's fun! Maybe they're sisters!"

"Maybe, but Fiona's dead now," I said.

Sloth sighed. "Well, that's less fun for sure. We should email Pamela."

I clicked the link for Pamela Arquette. Sloth's email program opened in response.

"What should we say?" I asked.

"Well, we could tell her we found a crappy map of historic Odyssey hidden in a laptop and we'd like her to take a look at it."

I shook my head. "I don't want anybody to know about the laptop," I said. "After all, people are already dead over it."

Sloth nodded her agreement. "Okay, then let's just tell her we're on this show, and the network asked us to investigate Odyssey's roots. You know, as a human-interest story or whatever."

I shrugged. "It's as good a reason to ask for a meeting as any." I quickly tapped out a message asking for an appointment and hit send.

"So, where were you and Envy off to so early this morning?"

I handed Sloth her phone back. "Remembrance Home. We were supposed to investigate talking corpses. But when we got there, the proprietor had been murdered."

Sloth squinted at me, tilting her head sideways. "Hmm. Now that you mention it, you do look a little shaken."

"Well, that tracks," I said. "It was unexpected, to say the least. It's not like people get murdered every day."

Sloth smiled. "You're so naïve sometimes," she said. "People do get murdered every day. Though in Odyssey, it only seems to happen about once a week."

Later that evening, there was a knock at my door. Before I could answer, Envy stepped into my room, closing the door softly behind her. Her hands on her hips, Envy tipped her chin upward, turning her face from side to side. "Okay, so let me have it. What do you think? Is it embarrassingly obvious and desperate or do I just look refreshed?"

I frowned. "What do I think about what?"

Envy gestured to her face. "About my new look! I

know it's a bit dramatic. But the dermatologist encouraged me to experiment and I don't know, I think I kind of like it. But maybe I don't. I can't tell! What do you think?"

I didn't think anything. Envy looked the way she always did, except her face wasn't moving around as much. She was usually more expressive. But you can't tell someone you don't notice anything when they're asking how they look, so instead I said, "Yeah, it looks great."

Envy took a step toward me, her eyes narrowing in suspicion. "You have no idea what I got done today, do you?"

Caught red-handed, I heaved a sigh of relief. "Nope. You look the same. Mostly."

"No, I don't. Though I'm not surprised you didn't notice. You're not the most observant person on the planet, I guess." She sighed and plopped down next to me on the bed. "I got my lips injected. I wanted a fuller, poutier look. It's not full-on Angelina Jolie, but it's pretty good. And then I let the doctor talk me into a round of Botox. Do you think it makes me look younger?"

I squinted. "You looked plenty young before," I said. "Besides, I don't know why people are so obsessed with youth. What's so bad about looking your age?"

Envy huffed and tossed her hair from her face. "Well, of course *you* can say something like that. You're gorgeous! You don't even try to look good, and you still have everyone around here swooning over you. I mean, you practically have Lust wrapped around your little finger."

I blushed furiously and looked away. Every instinct was to argue with Envy since nothing she just said was true, especially the gorgeous part. No, especially the everyone swooning over me part. Okay, both were equally ridiculous. But at the mention of Lust, my throat went dry. Something *was* developing between me and Lust. Or at least, I'd thought so. But then I saw her cozying up to Greed, and I was no longer sure I was even on her radar. I still felt something for her, though *what* I felt exactly, I was unsure of. Romantic relationships were not my forte. In all my life, I'd had exactly one girlfriend, and she dumped me because I was an inattentive moron. I didn't want to get too involved with anyone until I had my feet under me again.

Of course, I was also familiar with the adage, the best way to get over someone is to get under someone new. But I wasn't ready for that, either.

Nevertheless, none of this was something I wanted to discuss with Envy. "So did you want to talk more about your dermatological adventures, or should we get down to work?" I asked.

Envy shrugged and dug out Edgar's phone, tossing it into my lap. "All right, Business McBusinessPants. All work and no play. You can have the honors."

I opened Edgar Thornton's phone and located his audio memos. They were listed in chronological order, so I started with the most recent memo, titled "Monica Stewart." I pressed play.

It was a woman's voice speaking. The recording wasn't great, and the corpse wasn't speaking loudly, but if I closed my eyes, I could just make out what she was saying.

"Discussion, Madison Summerland. Having difficulty getting ahold of M at Summerland Memorial. Natalie will continue to try to contact. Might be a good idea to send cookies as a soft intro. Ginger to call Bake Some Waves for prices. Discussion, City Hall. Still no word on blueprints. Wilson to acquire papers from JG office. Action items, cookies, blueprints."

I looked over at Envy. "What does this sound like to you?"

Envy scrunched up her nose. "Like every work meeting I've ever been to. Maybe that's the wrong audio file."

"It's labeled Monica Stewart. According to Danielle, she was one of the talking corpses."

"Well, maybe he accidentally recorded over it. Try the next one."

I nodded and tried the next file. This one was labeled "Jack Wilcox." I pressed play and immediately cringed. The man was shouting instead of using his inside voice. But other than that, the content was much the same:

"Discussion, Portia for mayor. Cameron Realty, conflict of interest? PC to file papers. Discussion, community support for JG office. Do we want to start collecting pro-PC talking points? Discussion, Karen McMurtry. New gossip, anything to worry about? Anything to use against JG? Action items, PC to file papers, PC to meet with KM."

I stopped the playback and cocked an eyebrow at

Envy. "This really does sound like meeting minutes. Maybe it's notes from the city council? I know Portia Cameron sits on the council."

Envy hrmmed and bit her lip. "Could be. Let's keep going."

The next file was labeled "Inez Montoya." I played it.

"Discussion, historical landmark. Anthony to add item to city council agenda to make Old Downtown a historical landmark. Discussion, member outings. We need to be more welcoming to new initiates. Might want to look into holding a meet and greet to set expectations. Perhaps cemetery tour? Discussion, initiation ceremony. Do we want to partner with Felix for coffee discounts? Status check, green. Action items, AT to protect our meeting space, protect Odyssey."

"Do city councils host initiation ceremonies?" Envy asked.

"Do they have meet and greets at cemeteries?" The more we listened, the less I understood. I navigated to the last file labeled "Freddie McIntyre" and hit play.

"The underground of the city is like what's underground in people. Beneath the surface, it's boiling with monsters. Discussion, new location. Wilson proposes City Hall for new location if we can get a friend or colleague into office. WB will ask Pam to order blueprints of emergency shelter. Outstanding questions, what are the dimensions for the room? Discussion, birthday party ideas for WB. Notes, WB is allergic to chocolate. The underground of the city is like what's underground in people. Beneath the surface, it's boiling with monsters."

Envy reached across my lap and tapped the Stop button. "Whoa, that one was different. What's that about the monsters?"

It was unsettling, but I didn't have any answers. I could see why Danielle was disturbed. Aloud, I said, "Why would a corpse wake up to relay this information to a mortician?"

Envy was chewing her lips, not quite meeting my gaze. "If you ask me, that's the wrong question."

"I didn't—okay. If that's the wrong question, what's the *right* question?"

Envy grinned wickedly. "Why would someone want to kill Edgar Thornton? And then, of course the real question—who?"

It was a moment before I saw where Envy was going with this. As she sat twisting her hands in her lap with her newly-plumped lips pressed together, I realized she was expecting me to say something, so I said the first thing that came to mind. "No."

Envy's face crumpled as much as the Botox would allow, and she folded her hands beneath her chin. "But *why?*"

"Well, to start, investigating Edgar's murder is not our task! We signed up to help Danielle unravel that talking corpses mystery. That's it."

"That was all *before,*" Envy said, rolling her eyes. "Things have changed. Everyone knows the local cops are idiots. They'll look in all the wrong places for the killer. Starting with investigating the most obvious suspect."

Despite myself, I said, "And who's the most obvious suspect in your opinion?"

Envy took a breath. "Danielle's brother, Tony. Think about it, Pride. We know he's having financial problems. And we also know Tony is poised to inherit half the business upon Mr. Thornton's death. He had motive *and* opportunity. The police will be all over it like bees on honey."

"But Edgar was his *father*," I objected.

"That doesn't mean anything," Envy snorted. "Haven't you heard of the Menendez brothers? Or Lizzie Borden? People kill their parents for money all the time."

I sat back, leaning my head against the wall. I wasn't so sure it happened all the time, but I took her point. "I see what you're saying. But let me guess—with all your profound experience, you don't think Tony Thornton did it."

Envy nodded excitedly, ignoring my sarcasm. "Exactly. While the police are busy investigating the totally wrong guy, you and I can find the real killer."

"But Envy, what about our *task*? Don't you want to win? We're only two people. We can only do so much."

Envy threw up her hands and let them fall into her lap. "Well…maybe our task and the murder are related."

"And maybe they're not." I sighed and rubbed my eyes. "Envy, let's just focus on the corpses, okay? Let's be smart and let the police do their job."

"That's just it, Pride," she said, sliding off my bed and heading for the door. "I'm not like you. I'm not a thinker. I'm a feeler. And I *feel* like I don't care about talking corpses when a man is dead."

And before I could think of anything encouraging to say, she was gone.

I sighed, closing my eyes. I knew I was doing the right thing.

So why did I feel like a chump?

four

. . .

Long after the rest of the house was snoring away peacefully, I lay awake in bed, staring at the ceiling. I couldn't sleep. I glanced over at the clock; 3 a.m. I heaved out a sigh and sat up, throwing my legs over the side of the bed. I stood, stuck my feet into a pair of porcupine slippers I'd inherited from Envy, and trudged downstairs for a glass of warm milk.

As I waited for my milk to warm in the microwave, I listened to the deep silence of the house. I thought I could hear the surf lapping against the shore, but it was probably just the ambient buzz of electricity. Sinful House was really a sound stage at its heart, and there were hidden cameras and mics everywhere. Even when you were alone, you weren't really alone. Which isn't as comforting a thought as you might think.

When the milk was ready, I took my refreshment outside to the front lawn. I settled into a plastic yard chair and stretched my legs. From my vantage point, I could only see the Star of the Sea's back. But although I couldn't see her face, I saw her hands were still pressed to her cheeks, so it was a good bet that she was still screaming.

As I sipped my warm milk, I wondered what it meant. Maybe nothing. Maybe something.

Now, I really could hear the surf. I closed my eyes and settled in, enjoying the cool air on my face. Peaceful moments at Sinful House were few, and I tried to enjoy them when I could.

"You know, they cast you as Pride, but they probably should've cast you as Scaredy McScaredyPants," a voice said.

Remember what I said about never really being alone? This was doubly true for me. Ghosts have absolutely no boundaries.

I turned to see the ghost girl who had been haunting me most of my life sauntering over, her hands on her hips. She sat down in the empty chair next to mine, pulling her knees to her chest. She wrapped her arms around her legs and pulled them close. "You are the biggest scaredy pants I've ever met."

"Scaredy McScaredyPants?" I said. "Did you get that from Envy?"

The ghost girl smiled. "She says stuff like that a lot, doesn't she? I like her."

I nodded. "Well, you would. She's a schoolteacher. She probably has a lot of experience with kids. I guess you could sense that about her."

But the ghost girl shook her head. "No, that's not why I like her. I like her because she's brave. She sees a job that needs to get done, and she won't let anything stand in her way. She's unstoppable."

I chuckled. "Unstoppable? I don't know if I'd go that far."

The ghost girl lifted her chin defiantly. "Well, I would. Since she's lived here, she's tried her best to make everyone else around her happy. That's why she summoned that water elemental. Because you guys are all slobs." She said this while gesturing to the shovels Wrath and Greed left lying in the front yard. "It wasn't her fault that the water elemental went crazy and started destroying Sloth's bedroom. The smoke elemental wasn't her fault, either. Gluttony was upsetting her because he didn't believe in feng shui. Envy just wanted to create good energy in the house. Not just for herself, but for everyone. And even the earth elemental was her way of helping you with the shopping for your task."

I grunted, but the ghost girl was right. Envy's heart was always in the right place, even if her tactics didn't always work out so great. "I have a feeling you're going somewhere with this," I said.

"The whole reason you're in Odyssey is because a bunch of weird stuff happens here that only you and the other Sins can help with. Envy takes that seriously. And don't you think Danielle and her mother deserve to know why poor Mr. Thornton was killed?"

I took a long, slow drink of my milk. "Of course they deserve closure," I said. "But it's not my job to mete out justice for the whole world. Everyone has to pick their battles. And I'm choosing not to pick battles that will pit me against the local police. I just want to walk the straight and narrow."

"Why? You broke into a *morgue* to see what happened to Walt. And *he's* a bad guy!"

"Well, I didn't know that at the time," I muttered.

The ghost stared at me a while. Then she said, "That statue got into your head, didn't it? You're worried about disaster and bad luck, aren't you?"

Now that the ghost had said it aloud, I realized two things: One, it was ridiculous, and two, it was true. I was just starting to get comfortable in my new life. I had a nice place to live, people who tolerated me, and a purpose I felt good about. Things were looking up…and then a wandering statue showed up on my lawn and threatened to turn everything upside down. The last thing I needed was to go off-script with a bad luck omen staring me in the face. I just wanted to play the game, win my task, and move on.

But even as I thought this, I knew I was kidding myself. Envy was right: the police were known to be incompetent. And Edgar Thornton's story *did* deserve to be told.

"Envy and I are already in trouble with the network," I explained. "That stupid incident with the earth elemental at the grocery store has us on thin ice. I can't risk getting in trouble with the police after that. And like it or not, I don't have permission to get involved with an ongoing murder investigation."

The ghost girl spread her hands before her. "Well… why don't you just ask for permission?"

I opened my mouth to respond but quickly closed it

again. Then I sat there blinking like a moron. Because, actually, I hadn't thought of that. "Do you think they'd have me?" I asked.

The ghost girl tucked a lock of hair behind an ear. "I don't know. I'm just a kid. You're the grown-up. What do you think?"

"I don't know, either," I admitted. "They say it's better to ask for forgiveness than permission. But I'm not really an ask for forgiveness kind of person."

"You're really not," the ghost agreed. "Did you know that a newborn Chinese water deer is so tiny, you can basically hold it in one hand?"

I cocked an eyebrow at the change in subject. "A Chinese water deer? I've never heard of that. I think you made it up."

The ghost shook her head. "I didn't. And when they grow up, instead of growing antlers, they grow long front teeth. That's why they call it the vampire deer."

"Now I know you're making that up," I laughed.

"I'm not! Cross my heart. And did you know rats can't vomit, and that's why it's so easy to poison them?"

I snorted and finished my milk. "I didn't know that," I said. "I'm surprised that after all this time, you haven't run out of animal facts."

The ghost girl smiled brightly. "I'll never run out," she said. "No matter how long you're here on earth, you learn something new every day. Even scientists are finding out new things about animals all the time."

I smiled and leaned back in my seat, crossing my legs. "Is that right?"

The ghost girl shrugged. "I don't know. It's probably true."

We were quiet for a long stretch, the ghost girl humming to herself as I watched the statute, looking for some sign to indicate what she wanted from us. But the statue didn't move. I must have fallen asleep at some point because I woke up when my chin dropped to my chest. Taking that as the only sign I would get tonight, I got to my feet and stretched. "I guess I'll turn in," I said to the ghost girl. "You gave good advice tonight."

"I know," she said, her spectral form already fading into the night. "I always give good advice. Sometimes, you're even smart enough to take it."

And then she was gone.

five

. . .

T he next day, I headed down to the precinct.

On the way over, I rehearsed what I would say. It wasn't like I could just walk in and ask to be put on the Edgar Thornton murder case. If I knew one thing about cops, they didn't like to ask for help. I understood that better than anyone. So I needed to make it look like they were doing *me* a favor. That's why I allowed my sidekick, Beefy Camera Guy, to come with me. If I gave the cops a story about how the network wanted to do a fluff segment on my past as a para-normal investigator, they might be more willing to give me an inch.

It was the best I could come up with, anyway.

When I arrived, the station was mostly empty. A woman in uniform sat behind the desk drinking a cup of coffee. She gave me a disinterested look from behind her mug. "How can I help you?" she asked.

I tried on my best smile, the one I'm told is some-times pretty charming. I stuffed my hands into my pockets and said, "Do you know who the lead investigator on the Edgar Thornton case is?"

The desk officer shuffled through some papers scattered on her desk. Then, finding what she was looking for, she tapped the form with a finger and said, "That's Detective Kelly Doyle."

I stretched my smile. "Great. Is she in? May I speak with her?"

The desk officer grunted. "*He* isn't available right now, but if you call and…"

The officer stopped speaking mid-sentence as the front door opened and someone swept into the station, bringing with her the strong scent of perfume. I turned to see who the officer was frowning at.

The woman striding through the front door was Portia Cameron.

Portia walked right up to the desk, edging me out of the way without actually acknowledging my presence. She folded her hands on the counter and leaned forward, her smile made of ice. "April, you were supposed to have security at my house 20 minutes ago. Where is my security detail?"

April blinked, looking from Portia to me and then back again. "I'll be with you in just a minute, Portia," she said. "I was just helping, uh…" She gestured toward me vaguely, her mouth twisted into a little moue.

"Pride," I said. Every time I used that cockamamie name, it got a bit easier. "You were saying? About Detective Doyle?"

April leaned forward onto her elbows, her expression

skeptical. "And what do you want to talk to Detective Doyle about?"

"Isn't it obvious?" I asked. "I want to talk to him about the Edgar Thornton case."

"Well, if you think you know something, we have a tip line. However—"

"I don't need the tip line," I interrupted. "I want to lend my services."

April laughed, her eyes widening. "You want to help the detective on the case? Who even are you?"

I could have kicked myself. This was the opposite of what I had rehearsed. Not even five minutes into this ordeal and I'd already screwed it up.

But before I could drag myself out of the hole I'd just dug for myself, Portia cleared her throat and elbowed me aside. "April, this really can't wait. I'm supposed to have an escort to my meeting in San Leonardo. Remember? We talked about this. You said you would send two uniformed officers to my house. But nobody showed up, and no one has called."

April held up a finger. "You'll have to wait a minute, Portia. Pride and I aren't quite finished talking yet, are we, Pride?" She fluttered her lashes at me in a most un-officer-like way. "I assure you, we have the city's best detectives working the Thornton case. If you want the number for the tip line—"

"There's a paranormal aspect to the case," I said, the words rushing out before I could rein them in. As soon as I heard them aloud, I wanted to slap myself in the face. But there was no going back now, so what the heck? I went all in. "I'm not at liberty to discuss the details, but unless Detective Doyle can talk to ghosts, he might miss some important information only I can provide."

Portia turned on her heel to face me, her lips pursed. "Something about the Thornton murder is supernatural?" she asked, her eyebrow arched. "Are you sure?"

"No, I'm not sure," I admitted. "But I have reason to believe—"

"Is it possible the murderer has supernatural abilities? Or is somehow—to use your word—paranormal?"

I thought about Envy's suggestion that the talking corpses and the murder were related. Then I mentally played through the voices I'd heard on Mr. Thornton's phone. That weird line about underground monsters echoed through my brain, and a chill ran down my spine. "Yes, it's possible," I said.

Portia looked me up and down with a new expression—not quite interest, but a step or two above disdain, anyway. "Do you have experience working with the police?"

"Yes," I said again. "I worked with the San Diego police for several years. Detective Hidalgo and I—"

Now April's hand flew to her mouth, and her eyes went wide as she gasped. "Hold on a sec! You're Sid Sheridan, aren't you?"

I cast a sideways glance at the camera guy. They would have to edit the segment later. We weren't supposed to use our real names on the show, even though everyone knew who I was, thanks to being the only survivor of the Sam Lovelace fiasco. "Yes. I'm Sid Sheridan, paranormal investigator. And I'm here to offer my services to Detective Doyle to help solve the Edgar Thornton case."

April was still staring at me like she'd just seen a movie star when Portia grabbed me by my arm and tugged me around the officer's desk and deeper into the station. Over her shoulder, she called, "I'll take care of this, April. You get on the phone and send those officers to my home immediately, or I will call Chief Ramsey myself. Don't make me badmouth you to your boss." Under her breath, she muttered, "Police efficiency at its finest. I'm so glad to see my tax dollars at work."

I tried to object, but Portia wasn't listening as she tugged me down the hall. She led me to a door marked "Detective Kelly Doyle" and stopped, turning to face me. "I'm the most influential person in Odyssey," she said. "Not even the mayor has the connections I do. This is *my* town. And if there's one thing I can't stand, it's watching my career go down the toilet because some superstitious simpletons think my town is full of ghosts and shapeshifters. Do you have *any* idea what that could do to real estate prices?"

"This town *is* full of ghosts," I said, crossing my arms in defiance. "I'm not sure yet about the shapeshifters." I gestured toward the cameraman with a lift of my chin. "Portia, the town's supernatural tendencies are already well-known. It's all over television, for crying out loud." I sighed, blowing out my cheeks. "So, is this the part where you tell me to take my cameras and go home or else?"

Portia hesitated, the muscles in her jaw going taut. Her blue eyes went dark as a cloud passed over her features. I could almost see the gears in her brain whirring. Then she lifted her chin and sniffed. "No," she said finally. "Believe me, I would rather threaten you than ask for your help. I have a duty to protect Odyssey's reputation as safe for commerce, development, and investment. But instead…" She lowered her voice and stepped closer to me. "If Edgar Thornton's murder does have supernatural connections, I want you to prove it. Find the people responsible. Promise me. Promise me you'll find them."

I didn't want to promise Portia Cameron anything, not even when our interests aligned. She was a snake in the grass waiting to strike, and I didn't trust her further than I could throw her. But I suspected I needed her influence to get on this case.

Plus, there was a note of something in her voice that gave me pause. Something that sounded eerily close to sorrow.

I sighed, blowing out my cheeks. "I promise I'll do my best to expose the truth," I said. "But I'm not on your team, Portia. I'm on Edgar's team. Danielle's team. So if you tell me you're on *their* side, then you've got a deal."

Portia's eyes narrowed, but her lips cracked a smile. "You're not as dumb as you look," she said. "Okay. You do your job. Find the truth. And if that truth happens to look strange from the corner of your eyes, dig deeper." She pushed open the door to the detective's office. "Let's make you a paranormal investigator again."

———

Walking into Detective Doyle's office, a wave of nostalgia washed over me. How many times had I walked into Detective Hidalgo's office to discuss a case or go over evidence? It was a comforting feeling, walking into a room and knowing you would be helpful. But now, things were different. Detective Kelly Doyle was not Detective Aaron Hidalgo.

Not by a long shot.

Detective Hidalgo was barrel chested and broad shouldered, with dark, weathered skin, a salt-and-pepper beard, and a ready smile. He laughed big and smiled hard. In contrast, Detective Kelly Doyle looked like a private investigator from a black-and-white 1940s noir film. He was elegant and thin, with oiled blue-black hair combed away from his face. He had a sharp nose and a square jaw with a 5 o'clock shadow, even though it was still morning. He wore a plain white button-down shirt with the top button undone. He sat away from his desk, legs crossed, manicured fingers laced casually in his lap as he squinted at us. He was as different from Detective Hidalgo as night from day.

Portia put her hand on the small of my back and pushed me forward, gesturing toward a chair before the detective's desk. "Have a seat," she said with a smile. She took the chair next to mine, crossing her legs and folding her hands in her lap. She offered a frosty smile to the detective who had still not greeted us. "I brought you a visitor," she said.

Detective Doyle studied me, his expression utterly blank. Then his eyes flicked to Portia, and he adjusted in his seat, re-crossing his legs and clearing his throat. "What are you doing here, Portia?"

Portia leaned back, her foot bouncing lazily. "I understand you're the lead investigator on the Edgar Thornton case."

The detective dipped his chin in small acknowledgment. "I am," he said.

"Terrible what happened to Edgar. I can't imagine what his wife must be feeling. Tell me, have you spoken to Mrs. Thornton? How is she holding up?"

The detective studied Portia with the same empty stare he'd given me. "She's doing as well as one can expect. She lost her husband of 50 years. I imagine it's been a shock."

Portia nodded. "Indeed. Do you have any suspects?"

The detective chuckled, leaning his head to the side. "You know I can't discuss the details of an ongoing investigation with you, Portia. So why don't you cut the bull and tell me what you want?"

Portia reached over and laid a gentle hand on my forearm. "I want to introduce you to someone. Pride here is one of the housemates on that reality show filming in town—*Sinful House*." She turned to me, her brows peaked. "You were America's Favorite Sin after the first airing, right?"

I lowered my eyes as my cheeks flamed red. "That doesn't count," I grumbled. "That was basically a fluke."

"In any case," Portia continued as though I'd said nothing, "Pride also used to work for the San Diego Police Department as a paranormal investigator."

"It's nice to meet you," I said, trying on my charming smile.

Detective Doyle scoffed, his gaze flickering toward me. I said nothing, bracing myself for the worst. In my experience, when you tell someone you're a paranormal investigator, you get one of three responses:

1. Politeness. These guys mutter something banal and gracious like, "Oh, isn't that fun" or "I once played Bloody Mary in the girls' bathroom in high school." This is a blow off. What they really mean is, "You're a complete nutjob to believe in that cockamamie nonsense, and I'm low-key embarrassed for you right now."

2. Fascination. These people get really excited and start firing off questions. "How did you get involved with that? How many ghosts have you seen? What do they look like? Have you ever been so scared you wet yourself?" These people hear "ghosts" and they think of stuff like *Amityville Horror* or *The Legend of Hell House*. They don't realize ghosts are mostly ordinary people who happen to lack a heartbeat.

3. Inexplicable hatred. These people treat you like you just kicked their dog. They hate you and everything you stand for, and there's no good reason for it. Maybe you inspire fear, or doubt, or maybe they think you worship the devil. Or maybe they're angry because they

> think you're taking advantage of poor
> schlubs who naively believe in the occult.
> Who knows? But these people will do
> everything within their power to reduce you
> to the nothing they already believe you to be.

I'll let you guess which bucket Detective Doyle fell into.

"I don't have anything to say to you," the detective said, his eyes narrowing as he summed me up. "And, frankly, I find people like you—people who prey on grieving families—sickening. If it were up to me, I'd haul you out of Odyssey by your ear and lock you up if you ever tried to return."

At my side, Portia chuckled, winding the string of pearls at her throat around a finger. "That's no way to talk to our guest, Kelly. Furthermore, it's no way to talk to your new partner."

The detective barked out his astonishment as he reclined further and clasped his hands behind his head. "You never cease to amaze me, you know that? Your audacity is absolutely *boundless,* isn't it? I know you've got half the city tucked in your pocket and the other half wound around your little finger. Good for you. Everybody needs a hobby. But you don't get to just walk in here and tell me I have a new partner. This isn't politics; it's police work. I have a job to do."

"Of course it's politics," Portia shot back. "Everything is politics. You want to catch bad guys. I want to preserve property values. We want the same thing, Kelly."

The detective leaned forward and slapped his hand on his desk. "No, *you* want what's good for Portia. I want what's good for Odyssey."

"Adding Pride to your team is what's good for Odyssey," Portia said. "You need someone with these talents."

"What for?" The detective's eyes were wide and filled with incredulity. "Ed Thornton wasn't killed by a demon or a monster or a wight. He was murdered by a human with a gun. There's no such thing as magic or psychics or life after death, okay? All this hocus pocus you're so worked up about *doesn't exist.*"

It seemed particularly obtuse to claim the paranormal didn't exist in a town with a wandering statue and a Chinese restaurant staffed with incorporeal entities, but I figured it best not to say so.

Portia glared at the detective. "Then explain Peyton," she said quietly.

Something passed between the two of them, but I didn't have the context to know what. Finally, the detective sucked his teeth and turned to face me. "What's *your* angle? What are you hoping to get out of this? Money? Information on the family? I know you're not here out of the goodness of your heart."

This was the very moment I'd been preparing for. Clearing my throat nervously, I gestured toward the camera guy and said, "It's for the show."

The detective blinked. "You want to help investigate a murder for your *show?*"

I nodded. "Yes. Like Portia said, I used to work for the San Diego Police Department. The network wants to do a segment on my life before I came to Sinful House. They thought showing me back on the streets would, you know, make me more relatable to the viewers."

The detective scoffed and shook his head. "Right. Well, humor me a second, will you? Why do you think the Ed Thornton case needs paranormal investigation in the first place? From where I sit, the shooting looks pretty cut-and-dried."

"You think it was Tony Thornton, don't you?" Portia asked, a devilish twinkle in her eye. "You are so predictable. I swear, if I—"

"Shut up, Portia," the detective cut in. "Really. Just shut up." Detective Doyle looked at me again. "Well?"

Now I had a choice to make. I wasn't really at liberty to talk about the talking corpses, but if I didn't let the detective in on this information, my involvement in the case wouldn't make any sense at all. I took a breath and said, "Mr. Thornton's daughter, Danielle, suspects Remembrance Home might be haunted. She contacted the show to ask us to look into it."

The detective nodded. "So you think the haunting— your word, not mine—and the murder are related?"

I shrugged. "I don't know, to be honest. But it seems an angle worth looking at."

Detective Doyle's brow furrowed as he considered this. "What *exactly* do you propose, Pride?"

"Let me work the haunting angle alongside your murder," I said. "If my investigation turns up any evidence relevant to your case, I promise to hand it over to you. And if you find anything that might help me…"

I shrugged. "You'll do me the same courtesy. It's a grieving daughter's wish," I added, hoping I wasn't overplaying my hand.

The detective sighed heavily as he leaned back into his chair. He looked from me to Portia, who was grinning like she knew she'd just won whatever game we were playing. Finally, the detective said, "One way or another, I'll have to agree to this, won't I? If I say no, I'll just get a call from the chief telling me to reexamine my priorities. Isn't that right?"

Portia leaned her head to the side. "It's almost like you're a psychic yourself, Kelly. You have an uncanny ability to predict the future."

The detective glared at Portia and then turned that same anger to me. "I'll let you know when it's safe to visit the crime scene," he said. "Anything else?"

I hesitated. "I may need to talk to some people. But like I said, if I find out anything, you'll be the first to know."

Detective Doyle snarled at me. "Sure, no problem! Contaminate my witnesses all you want. Portia here doesn't mind, and everyone knows she runs this city. Right?"

Portia just sat demurely, saying nothing.

I cleared my throat again. "I don't want to be an inconvenience. I just want to get to the bottom of this. So, I know it doesn't mean much to you, but I really appreciate it."

Detective Doyle scoffed. "You're right. Your appreciation means absolutely nothing to me."

Both Portia and I stood and moved toward the door.

With one hand on the knob, Portia looked over her shoulder. "It was nice seeing you again, Kelly. Please give your wife my love."

I heard the detective curse as we closed the door behind us.

In the hallway, I jerked my thumb over my shoulder. "What was all that about? Did the guy cut up your paper dolls when you were kids? You two act like you're mortal enemies or something."

Portia laughed as we headed to the front of the station. She gave April a parting glare as we walked out the front door and headed into the parking lot. "Well, of course Kelly and I are enemies," she said, opening the door to her silver BMW. "He's my ex-husband."

six

. . .

When I arrived back at Sinful House, I went immediately to Envy's room to tell her the good news.

I found her sitting at her desk, hunched over Edgar's phone, listening to an audio memo. When she saw me, she stopped the recording and pushed the phone away with a sigh. "I was looking for you," she said. "I've been listening to these recordings all morning. I still can't make heads or tails of them."

I sat at the foot of Envy's bed and nodded. "Yeah, they're confusing. That's okay, though. The messages might not be our only chance to find the truth."

Envy sat up straighter, her eyes going wide. "Really? Did you learn something? Where *were* you, anyway? I figured we'd get a jump start on the day, but when I went to your room, you weren't there."

I waved my hand, dismissing this concern. "Yeah, I had things to do this morning. But you'll be glad to hear what I was up to. I had a change of heart. Well, not a change of heart exactly. A change of perspective."

Envy rolled her hand in a "get on with it" motion, and I took a breath and pressed on. "Last night, I started thinking about everything you said. And you were right. We are uniquely qualified to help find Edgar Thornton's killer, assuming his murder had anything to do with the talking corpses. So I figured, why not just ask the police if we could help?"

Envy blinked, her expression dour. "Just ask them. You thought you could just *ask* the police to join an active investigation?"

The way she said it made it sound like the dumbest idea in the world. How come when the ghost suggested it, it sounded plausible? "Well, I just thought it couldn't hurt."

Envy leaned her chin into her hand, the fingers of her other hand drumming the desktop rhythmically. "So that's where you were? You went down to the police station behind my back?"

A tiny twinge of guilt slithered up my spine. "I wouldn't say that," I said. "I mean, I didn't go behind your back. That makes it sound like I purposefully left you out of it. In actuality, I just never thought to invite you along."

Envy snorted. "You know that's actually worse, right? I mean, that's totally way worse."

When I'd walked into this room, I was so excited to tell Envy the good news. Now, I felt like I was drowning in quicksand. This kind of stuff is why I prefer not to deal with people. "Well, think of it this way. What if they'd said no, and then you'd gotten your hopes up for nothing? This way, I could spare you the emotional rollercoaster."

Envy sighed, shaking her head as she leaned back and folded her arms over her chest. "Quit digging. You screwed up, but that's okay. It happens. Next time, don't forget about me. I'm your partner."

I made an X over my heart. "I won't," I solemnly swore.

Momentarily appeased, Envy's scowl evaporated and was replaced with a lovely smile. "Okay. So. What happened?"

I was so relieved she didn't ask for an apology that I nearly passed out. "Well, I met with the lead detective on the case. This guy Kelly Doyle. He's reluctantly agreed to let us look into the Thornton case. We have to promise to stay out of his way, and if we find anything promising, we have to turn it over to him immediately. But otherwise, we're good. We have free rein."

Without warning, Envy jumped from her seat and threw her arms around my neck, squealing in my ear as she hugged my head with all her might. "I can't believe this! That's so amazing! I mean, it was awful of you not to invite me along, but whatever, I forgive you. This is such great news, Pride!" She sat back down, her hands pressed to her mouth. "But now I don't know what to do. Like, where do we start?"

I leaned back into my hands, my brow furrowed. "One thing Detective Hidalgo taught me is sometimes you have to start with a story. A 'what if' situation. So let's try this. What if Edgar Thornton heard something from the corpses he wasn't supposed to hear? Or maybe someone *thought* he heard something he wasn't supposed to hear?"

"*Boring* information," Envy drawled, rolling her eyes. "I mean, those recordings are not exactly *Dear Diary* level stuff, you know? We heard everything Edgar heard, and…"

Envy gasped, her words stuttering to a stop. She covered her mouth again, her eyes growing round. "Wait a minute," she breathed. "When I played those memos, I was listening for something out of the ordinary. Something suspicious. But maybe the clue we need is in what's *not* recorded."

I frowned. "What are you talking about?"

Envy pointed to the phone. "When we found Mr. Thornton's body, there was another corpse in the preparation room, right? That woman Karen McMurtry. But there's no recording of her on the phone."

I blinked. I hadn't thought of that. "Go on."

"According to the cops, Karen was a busybody blabbermouth. If anyone in this town knew secrets and scandals, it was her. So what if the killer purposely struck before Karen woke up? It wouldn't keep Karen from talking—but it would keep anyone from listening."

"But like you said, all the corpses just recited meeting minutes." I objected. "So even if Karen did wake up, chances are she'd just be babbling about bake sales or something."

Envy shrugged. "If you were a killer with a secret, would you take that risk?"

I stared at Envy a moment, mulling over what she'd

said. It was a good starter scenario. I got to my feet and started pacing around Envy's room, my hands clasped behind my back. I always did my best hypothesizing on my feet. "That's not bad thinking, Envy. Good job. Okay. If you're right, we need to know who else knew about the corpses. Do you still have Danielle's phone number?"

Envy reached for Mr. Thornton's phone. "Danielle said her number is in here. Should I call her?"

I nodded. "Let's do it."

We put the phone on speaker and dialed. It rang for a while but eventually went to voicemail. "Hi, Danielle," my housemate cooed. "It's Envy. Call me back when you can. Pride and I have some questions for you. Please take care of yourself."

She disconnected and placed the phone back on the desk. "Well, what should we do while we wait for her to call us back?"

I hesitated, chewing my lips. "I have an idea," I drawled, "but you probably won't like it."

Envy donned a delighted expression and rubbed her hands together. "That sounds juicy. What is it?"

I took a breath. "We should have a chat with Karen McMurtry's partner in crime."

A heartbeat passed, then two. Finally, understanding dawned on Envy's face, and she groaned, folding over the desk in mock pain. "Oh, no. You think we should go talk to that awful woman with the newsletter? Stephanie Jones?"

I nodded. "She and Karen were thick as thieves, right? If Karen knew something murder-worthy, I'd bet dollars to donuts she told her blabbermouth friend about it."

Envy sat up, still frowning. "If you want, you can leave me behind just this once." A hopeful smile lit up her face.

I shook my head. "Nope. We're in this together. Come on, Envy. Let's go talk to your biggest fan. As long as you don't summon any little people, we should be fine."

She glowered at me as she climbed to her feet. "That's not funny, Pride."

I didn't respond to that. But I thought it was a little funny.

———

Stephanie Jones owned a pet grooming boutique in the heart of downtown Odyssey. The shop was named All Dogs Go to Odyssey. I think the name was supposed to be a cute pun or something, but it didn't make any sense. And I say that as someone who spent far too long trying to make sense of it because I hated it when other people got jokes and I was the only one who didn't. (That happened a lot.) The best I could come up with was maybe she was trying to compare Odyssey to heaven, but boy, was that ever a stretch. In any case, the name of the salon wasn't the only unfortunate thing about it.

The boutique catered especially to toy poodles. As soon as we walked in the door, we were greeted by the yipping and yapping of tiny purse dogs dyed every color of the rainbow. I'm not kidding. The whole place was set up like a beauty salon, with chairs, sinks, mirrors, stylists and everything. But instead of human clients, each stylist was working on a pooch. Puff balls ranging from pink to lavender to sky blue and sunshine yellow set barking and yapping in every corner of the salon. I wasn't a fan of tiny purse dogs. I was especially not a fan of tiny purse dogs that looked like cotton candy but acted like they wanted to chew my face off.

(I know how that *sounds*, but I'm not afraid of poodles. Not exactly. Whatever, I don't have to explain myself. Everybody has inexplicable fears.)

Stephanie Jones saw us as soon as we walked in. She scowled at us from behind the counter, dressed head to toe in black. She wore one of those old-fashioned pillbox hats with a little net veil that covered half her face. In addition, she wore a long-sleeved black silk blouse, a knee-length black skirt, and sensible black shoes. A mourning outfit. Amid the rainbow of pastel puff balls, she stood out.

We approached the desk, and Stephanie pursed her lips in disdain. "Well, do my eyes deceive me, or is it the local hoodlums come to pay me a house call? I don't suppose you have an appointment," she asked wryly.

I tried to look nonchalant, which is pretty rough when you're terrified of getting jumped at any moment by five-and-a-half pounds of pure fluffy fury. But I did my best. "Hi there, Stephanie. We don't have an appointment. We don't have any poodles, either," I added.

At my side, Envy squirmed uncomfortably. "Hi, Stephanie," she croaked.

Stephanie scoffed and pulled a face. "If you don't have any dogs that need grooming, why are you here?"

"We want to talk about Karen McMurtry."

Stephanie froze, real tears pooling in her eyes. She blinked quickly, trying not to let the tears fall, but I saw how the name affected her. She swiped her face with her fingertips and sniffed. "You're here to offer your condolences?" she asked, glancing toward the cameraman. "The network sent you, right? To ease the tension between us? I'm sure they're worried about ratings."

"Our condolences. Yes," I lied, recognizing an in when I saw one. "But the network didn't send us. We're neighbors, after all. All part of the Odyssey community. When one of us suffers, we all suffer." I must have picked up that schmaltzy malarkey from Dr. Xena. It wasn't something I would normally say.

Or maybe Envy was psychically inspiring me. I wasn't sure which I preferred.

My fake sympathy seemed to do the trick, however. Stephanie's expression softened as she nodded, her shoulders slumping in her grief. "Karen and I were peas and carrots," she breathed. "We've been friends since we were girls. We grew up next door to each other. We even dated each other's brothers at one point. No one was closer to Karen than me. No one."

I nodded. "If you don't mind my asking, how did she die?"

Stephanie reached into a pocket and retrieved a handkerchief to dab around her damp nostrils. "She had a heart condition and passed peacefully. And she will be missed every day by those who loved her." Stephanie covered her face with her hands and cried quietly into her palms.

I didn't say what I was thinking, which was that from what I could tell, no one loved Karen McMurtry. Even the cops at Remembrance Home practically high-fived her death. Instead, I said, "Stephanie, did Karen have secrets she didn't share with you?"

Stephanie looked up, blinking. She wore an expression I couldn't read when she said, "Karen's secrets? I'm sure she did, yes. Everyone does."

"No, that's not what I mean." I paused to rephrase the question. "I mean, did Karen have dirt on other people that she didn't share with you? Maybe something, I don't know…like blackmail?"

Envy kicked me and shot me a glance, but I ignored her. I was working on pure instinct, throwing darts in the dark. I just hoped Envy's ability would land me a bullseye.

Stephanie sniffled and shook the hair from her face. "Blackmail? That's such a dirty word. It sounds so salacious. Well, I don't know about blackmail, but Karen knew compromising things about everyone, of course."

"Even you?"

Stephanie pressed her lips into a hard line. "Well, I…Excuse me, but why are you asking? I thought you were here to offer condolences!"

"We are," Envy cut in, her voice as soft as butter. "I know what it's like to lose a friend. Girlfriends mean so much to each other, don't they? You've lost your closest confidante. We thought you might want to talk about her." Envy fluttered her lashes and put on her most angelic smile. Really, she was pretty good at this whole dealing-with-grieving-blabbermouths thing. Especially considering how much she didn't like Stephanie.

Stephanie swallowed, new tears forming in her eyes. "Everyone in this town is treating me like a leper," she admitted. "They're avoiding me so they *don't* have to offer condolences. They hated her, you know? Because she called things like she saw them. But she was my dear friend. Do you know how hard it is to grieve alone?"

"I do," Envy said. "No one should have to grieve a friend by themselves. So do you? Want to talk about it?"

Stephanie chewed her lips, considering. She glanced around the salon to ensure no one could overhear our conversation. Then she stepped out from behind the desk and took Envy by the arm. "Let's talk outside," she said.

Envy and I followed Stephanie out into the sunshine. The day was clear and bright without a cloud in the sky. A gentle breeze blew, and I heard the scream of seagulls overhead.

"Karen liked to gossip, it's true," Stephanie said as soon as the door to the salon closed behind us. "But she was more than just a gossip. She had a big heart. That's why she helped me with the newsletter. I don't have the nose for news that Karen did," she admitted. "Karen had a gift. And she willingly and *lovingly* shared important news with the community. Although," she added, "she didn't always share *everything*. Even Karen knew some information shouldn't be disclosed."

Envy and I exchanged a glance, and my heart rate picked up. This sounded exactly like the kind of clue we were looking for. All we had to do was keep Stephanie talking. And Envy was apparently great at that.

"You and Karen were both doing good work, you know," Envy said. "Protecting the community and everything."

Stephanie linked her arm in Envy's, and the two fell into a rhythm, their steps aligning. "Protecting the community! Yes! See, you get it. When we ran that story about you, for example, the purpose wasn't to hurt you. It was to protect Odyssey from bigotry and bullying."

Envy hrmmed in tacit agreement, though I knew she had to be thinking the same thing I was, which was, "What a crock." But if Envy wasn't gonna call her on it, neither was I.

"I imagine she took a lot of secrets to the grave," Envy pressed on.

"I'm sure she did," Stephanie agreed. "And as sad as I am about her passing, it does give me some small relief, if I'm being honest."

Envy tipped her head. "Why?"

Stephanie looked pensive as the ocean breeze ruffled her hair. Her little black veil fluttered in the wind, casting web-like shadows across her tear-stained face. "Sometimes, I worried for her physical safety," she said finally, the words sounding like they came straight from a confessional. "She knew things she shouldn't, and there were people in this town who weren't beyond threats. If you know what I mean."

My heart did a cartwheel. "Threats? Someone

threatened her?"

"Oh, all the time," Stephanie guffawed, nodding enthusiastically. "Like I said, she knew things she shouldn't. I worried sometimes that she'd share the wrong secret and someone would hurt her. One person in particular."

Envy stopped short, her face imploring. "Who? Stephanie, who wanted to hurt your friend?"

Stephanie looked around nervously, her fingers worrying the delicate studs on her ears. She chewed her lip, eyes flickering here and there. "This is really…I could get in trouble," she whispered.

"We won't tell a soul," Envy whispered. To the camera guy, she called out, "Please put that away. In fact, can you give us some space?"

I expected an objection, but Beefy Camera Guy merely lowered the camera to his side and backed away a respectful distance. I eyed Envy with a new level of respect. My housemate took Stephanie's hand in her own and said, "Tell me."

Stephanie was silent a long time. Then she nudged Envy forward, and we were walking again. "This happened years ago, so forgive me if I don't remember all the details. Karen and I were making a birthday cake in my kitchen when my phone rang. It was Charmaine Young. Do you know Charmaine?"

I nodded. "Sure. She's an actress, right? Played Titania in the most recent ORCA production."

Stephanie nodded. "That's the one. Anyway, she was calling because it had finally happened. Charmaine got her first big audition. She'd been trying to land a Hollywood gig for as long as I can remember. But between you, me, and the fence post, she's only a mediocre actress, so her career wasn't going anywhere. So landing an honest-to-goodness audition was a huge deal. She wanted me to put it in my newsletter. I told her I'd love to interview her for my article, but I was up to my elbows in frosting and couldn't do her justice at the time. But I was being sneaky, see. I really was excited for Charmaine. So I sent Karen to her house to do a surprise interview. You know, like a paparazzi thing. I thought it would be fun to surprise her. But after what happened next, maybe that wasn't the best idea I ever had."

I slowed my pace. "And why is that?"

"Karen sneaked into the backyard through the side gate. She heard splashing in the pool, so she figured Charmaine was celebrating by doing a few laps. Charmaine loves to swim. She was a champion in high school. Anyway, Karen sneaked around to the pool with her camera in hand. But when she got to the pool, she saw…something."

I stopped dead in my tracks as my heart seized and my blood ran cold. I held up a hand, and both Stephanie and Envy halted. "What did she see?" I asked.

"I don't know," Stephanie said, her voice hard as nails. "I don't know, and Karen wouldn't tell me. What I do know is Charmaine grabbed Karen and knocked the camera from her hands and kicked it into the pool. Then she told Karen if she told anybody what she saw, she'd kill her."

"That's pretty dramatic," Envy said. "But people say things like that all the time, right? I mean, as a kid, I told my brother if he told anybody I had to wear headgear at night, I'd kill him."

Stephanie swallowed hard, wringing her hands as we began walking again. "No, you don't understand. Charmaine has a temper. She's an actress, so she's good at hiding it. But I've known Charmaine for years. She could get hot, you know. Violent. Karen said when she looked in Charmaine's eyes, she knew she meant it. If she ever told anyone what she had seen, Charmaine really would kill her." She shook herself, her bottom lip folded under her teeth. "I've never told anyone that story," she said. "Not a soul. I never ran the piece in the newsletter about Charmaine's audition, either. It just didn't seem right. Especially since she didn't get the part."

We'd made our way around the block and were now headed back toward the salon. With the building in view, Stephanie unlinked her arm from Envy's, her spine straightening. "Well, thank you for your visit," she said, "but I need to get back to work. Please, don't tell anyone any of this, okay?"

I thought it was pretty rich for the gossip queen to beg us for discretion, but I didn't say so. "Your secret is safe with me," I said.

"And me," said Envy.

"And me," said Beefy Camera Guy.

Stephanie pinched her lips and strode purposefully into the salon, the door swinging silently closed behind her.

seven

. . .

O nce we were in the car, Envy turned to me and rubbed her hands together excitedly. "I'd say that was successful! We have our very first suspect! If Charmaine threatened to kill Karen to keep a secret, she might kill Edgar to keep that same secret, right? Should we go question Charmaine?"

I nodded and put the car into gear. "She's definitely on our list. But first, I'd like to speak to Danielle and find out if Charmaine knew about the talking corpses. Because if she didn't know, she has no motive."

Envy made a thinking sound in her throat. "That's not a bad idea, but I think you're being a little short-sighted."

I quirked an eyebrow in her direction. "How do you mean?"

"Well, if Danielle says *no one* else knew about the corpses, that's one thing. But if she says even one person knew, then we have no idea how many people actually knew."

"We don't?"

"Didn't you even go to high school?" Envy asked, incredulous. "Okay, look. It's like this: the likelihood of a secret getting out is equal to the square of the number of people who know the secret. So, let's say Danielle only told one person. That's three people that know: Danielle herself, Edgar Thornton, and the mystery person. Right? The square of three is nine. So if she only told one person, we're actually looking at a total of nine people who might know it."

I hrmmed, unconvinced. "Well, why stop there? If nine people know the secret, couldn't they tell someone, and then *they'd* tell someone, until the whole world knows the secret?"

"Mathematically, sure," Envy agreed. "But at some point, you run out of people close enough to the secret to care. No one cares about the friend of a friend of a friend of a friend who had an affair. It's got to be intimate to mean something."

I grunted noncommittally. Although Envy's logic added up, I wasn't sure where she got the equation from in the first place. (I did go to high school, but my friends weren't the gossiping sort. Or maybe I just wasn't the person others gossiped to. On further speculation, that's rather likely. I was probably the one they were gossiping *about*.) Still, it did make a very human kind of sense. People—even leaving aside the Stephanies and Karens of the world—liked to talk. So even if Danielle only told one person, there was no guarantee that person didn't tell someone else and so on and so on.

Honestly, now that I was thinking about it, it made me never want to tell anyone anything ever again.

"Fine, I see where you're going with this. But in the meantime—"

I was interrupted by the buzzing of my phone.

I answered, holding the phone to my ear with my shoulder. "Hello?"

The voice on the other end was breathy. "Pride! Great, so glad I caught you. It's Sloth. Are you busy right now?"

"Not really. Why?"

"Pamela Arquette just emailed me back. The woman from the historical society. She's at City Hall right now. I thought you might want to meet me there."

I glanced over at Envy in the passenger seat and let the phone drop away from my mouth. "Hey Envy, do you have anywhere you need to be? I need to meet Sloth at City Hall. Is that okay?"

Envy's phone rang then, and she held up a finger. "Hang on, it's Greed." Into the phone, she said, "Yeah? Uh huh. *Really?* Yes, awesome! Okay, thank you so much. You're the best." She disconnected and slipped her phone away. "I've got no plans."

I spoke into the receiver again. "Okay, I'll meet you in 10 minutes."

I thumbed the phone off and put it aside. "What did Greed want?"

"To talk to me," Envy answered with an evasive smile.

"About what?"

She giggled. "Nunya."

I knew this joke, so I let it drop and rolled my eyes. "You are such a child sometimes," I said.

"And you're nosy. So what's going on at City Hall?"

She had some nerve calling me nosy and then asking about my business. But I was bringing her along for the ride, so I guess she had a right to ask. I sucked in a breath, my eyes drifting to the rear-view mirror. "Sloth and I are looking into the history of Odyssey," I said to the camera guy. "But it's strictly off-camera. No footage. I'm dropping you off on the corner. You can take a rideshare back to the house."

Beefy Camera Guy shrugged his huge shoulders. "That's fine. It's a nice day out. Just let me out here; I'll walk."

I was already preparing my mouth to counter his argument when I realized he wasn't arguing. Maybe this new camera guy would actually work out. I pulled over, and the camera guy climbed out of the back seat, leaving his equipment behind. He flashed me a peace sign and said, "Catch you later."

Envy pressed her forehead to the window, watching him as he walked the opposite direction. "He's kind of cute, isn't he?" she said. "He's got a cute butt."

If there was one thing I wasn't going to talk about, it was Beefy Camera Guy's butt. "Listen, Envy. I need to tell you something."

I quickly explained the details of the Eleanor Romanowsky case as I drove the rest of the way to City Hall. Not everything, but enough to get her up to speed on the murder, Chenoweth, the laptop, and the map I'd found inside. "So that's why we're meeting with Pam

Arquette," I concluded. "We're hoping she can tell us something about the local cemeteries. Assuming the star on the map marks graves, which is what Sloth and I both think, it could be a big clue."

Envy was quiet a moment before saying, "Eleanor was killed over a map?"

I nodded. "That's right," I said. "And that's why I had to tell you before I dragged you into this. It could be dangerous. So if you don't want to get involved, say the word. You can get a ride back to the house. Nobody would blame you."

Envy rolled her eyes and tossed her hair over her shoulder. "It's like you've never met me or something. All I want in life is adventure and excitement. I get so tired of all the Boring McBoringPants things I do every day. I'm not afraid of a couple faceless bad guys."

"They're bad guys with guns," I reminded her.

Envy looked out the window. "Everything worth doing costs something," she said. "No pain, no gain."

That was good enough for me. I parked the car and we got out.

———

Ten minutes later, we walked into Pamela Arquette's office at Odyssey City Hall.

Sloth was already there when we arrived. She was sitting on a loveseat across from an impressive-looking elderly woman with silver-white hair styled in a chignon with mother-of-pearl combs. She wore a perfectly tailored aubergine skirt suit and an eggshell blouse ornamented with a simple string of pearls. Her fingernails were elegantly manicured and painted a conservative nude color. When she saw Envy and me, she stood and donned what I could only call a politician's smile. She held out her hand and, though I'm usually hesitant to touch other people, I shook it happily.

"You must be Pride," the woman said with a smile. "I'm Pamela Arquette. It's so nice to meet you. I'm glad you were able to meet here at my office. I've been underwater lately."

I glanced around the ornately furnished room. "Are you…the mayor?"

Pamela laughed, a sound like bells chiming. "Goodness, no. Our mayor is Julian Gillespie. If you're going to live in Odyssey, you should know that," she said with a wink. "No, I'm the city manager." She turned to Envy. "I'm sorry, I don't believe I've had the pleasure. You are?"

Envy flushed a deep crimson and held out her own hand. "Envy," she said as they shook. "Nice to meet you, ma'am."

The older woman laughed and shook her head. "Please. This is California. Just call me Pam."

I sat down next to Sloth, and Envy took a chair beside Pam. When everyone was settled, Pam scooted to the edge of her seat, her hands folded neatly on her knees, and said to Sloth, "So what is the nature of your inquiry, dear?"

Sloth shot me a nervous look and cleared her throat. "Well, we wanted to know the history of Odyssey."

Pam smiled brightly, like a nine year-old-boy who

was just asked to explain the premise of his favorite video game. "All right. Well, that's a very broad topic. Where would you like to start?"

Sloth fingered the end of her pigtail, her mouth scrunched to one side as she thought. "Well, for starters, how old is this town? When was Odyssey founded?"

"1785. We are the second oldest city in California after San Diego." Pam's voice was rich with pride as she spoke. "Odyssey was one of the first Catholic missions located along El Camino Real. The city's original name was Santa Angela de la Cruz. The mission was run by two padres—Father Lucien Alvarez and Father Dante Figueroa. They are credited as the founders of Odyssey."

Sloth nodded and glanced over to me. "Are the padres…buried around here?"

I had to admire Sloth's segue into the topic we actually cared about. I wouldn't have thought her so capable. But maybe she was being affected by Envy's magic, too.

Pam nodded. "They are, in fact. They're both buried at Haven of Repose, our oldest cemetery. It's where our most notable citizens and founders are laid to rest. It's south of here, near the outskirts of town."

"Does Odyssey have many cemeteries?" I asked.

Pam's eyebrows lifted. "Not many, but a few. Are you looking for your progenitors? Do you have family that might be buried here?"

"No," I said. "All my family vanished."

Pam blinked in surprise, and Sloth tittered, her cheeks coloring pink. "Have you heard of the Sam Lovelace commune?" she asked.

"Of course. That artist colony up in Santa Barbara." Understanding swept over Pam's face, and she turned her wide, unblinking eyes on me. "You're the baby they found," she breathed. "The lone survivor. My heavens. A celebrity in our own midst!"

I felt my face flush hot. "It's really not that big a deal," I mumbled.

"Pride's also a ghost whisperer," Sloth said, warming up to the conversation. "So all this cemetery stuff is like, professional curiosity."

Pam stared at me a moment longer, her gaze penetrating. I held her eyes for as long as I could, but then I had to look away. It's mortifying to have someone stare at you like that. It's like they can see all your secrets. As though realizing what she was doing, Pam suddenly turned away, looking back to Sloth. "Well, I wouldn't say we have *many* cemeteries, but we have a number. My parents are buried at The Longest Night just up the road. We recently added a new cemetery only a few blocks from here—it's called Playa View Memorial Park." She turned her gaze to me once again. "As our very own ghost whisperer, would you be interested in hosting a haunted cemetery tour? I hear we have a number of citizens who would be interested in such a thing."

I had to school my face to keep from scowling. See, this is why I usually keep this stuff to myself. "Anything's possible," I hedged. Anything wasn't. I'd rather die than host a haunted cemetery tour.

"You should consider it," she said. "Odyssey is a very haunted city if you know where to look." Again, I had to bite my tongue to keep from laughing. I was well aware of Odyssey's ghost infestation. "In fact," Pam continued, "while we're dishing about ghosts, I'll share this with you. Every mission in California is said to be haunted, but our mission, the old Mission Santa Angela de la Cruz, was perhaps the most infamous. The story is that an indigenous medicine woman known only as Magdalena was accidentally killed and buried on mission property. At night, her soul wandered the city, looking for sick and injured to tend. Whenever her soul came upon someone close to death, she stayed with them and comforted them until they passed. Then she guided their soul back to the mission where she ministered to them until their soul was healed and could cross over into heaven. To this very day, the mission and the property it stood on is considered the very *heart* of Odyssey." She chuckled and offered a thin shrug. "If you go for that sort of thing."

Sloth opened her backpack and retrieved a piece of paper, handing it to Pam. "I think this is a rough map of Odyssey from 1902," she said. "None of the streets or buildings are marked, so I'm not sure what I'm looking at. Does this look at all familiar to you?"

I peered over Sloth's shoulder and noticed that the map Sloth handed Pam was not the same paper we'd found in the laptop. Sloth had reproduced it, leaving off the tell-tale star underneath the mounds. She also hadn't reproduced the weird phrase "Nexus of Power" or the title.

Pam studied the hastily drawn document, turning the paper this way and that. "Well, it's not exactly a work of art, is it?" she asked, giggling good-naturedly. "Oh, I hope that wasn't offensive. It wasn't your child that drew this, was it?"

"Our producer gave it to us," I said. The lie slid easily from my lips, and I threw a sideways glance at Envy, who smiled. This glibness had to be her doing. You know, if being in Envy's presence meant I always knew the right thing to say, maybe our partnership would work out great. "The history of Odyssey is for a segment the network wants to do. So do you recognize it?"

Pam tapped a finger against her chin and nodded. "Well, it's hard to tell, given the lack of…precision," she said, diplomatically. "But it looks like it could be a sketch of our original downtown."

That piqued my interest. "Downtown? Really?" I leaned forward and pointed to the map. "So those half oval shapes—could they refer to a nearby cemetery? Maybe the one you said was only blocks away?"

Pam shook her head. "Playa View wasn't around in 1902," she said. "But anyhow, those aren't graves. Those are mission archways. Here, let me show you."

Pam rose to her feet and strode across the office to her bookshelf where she retrieved a large, hardbound coffee table book titled, *A Photographic History of Spanish Southern California*. She returned to her seat, flipping the book open on her lap. "Here. See this?" She pointed to a black and white photograph of an adobe-tiled building where a series of curved archways formed a long outdoor corridor. "This is what the California missions looked like. Spanish architecture featured these curved doorways and windows frequently. Many early maps used those arches to indicate a mission."

I stood to get a better look at the book. Peering over Pam's shoulder, I said, "Interesting. I never noticed any mission downtown, though. What happened to it?"

"I'm not sure exactly," Pam admitted. "It disappeared ages ago. But for a long time, we had a museum here honoring the mission and Odyssey's early history. It was small, but it housed some sacred relics from the old mission, including Magdalena's grave marker. And if I'm reading this map right, these arches align to where the museum would have been."

My heart was thundering away in my ears, and I had to swallow down my excitement. "And what's there now?"

Pam shrugged. "Well, now we call it Old Downtown. It's a very quaint, very trendy area. There's a nail salon, a day spa, and a lovely little café called Déjà Brew. There's been some talk about designating the area a historical landmark so it can't be further developed. I'm in favor, of course, but not everyone is. It's a heated issue around town."

A disembodied voice drifting through the room interrupted my oncoming epiphany. "Yes, I'll take two of those. Just put it on my card."

I looked around quickly, scanning for the ghost that must have appeared. I didn't recognize the voice—it belonged to a man, booming and clear. But it didn't take long to realize the others heard the voice, too, so it couldn't be a ghost. I opened my mouth to ask what was happening when Pam sighed, stood, walked over to the wall, and pounded on it three times.

"The acoustics in these old buildings are notoriously mysterious," Pam explained, a chagrined smile on her lips. "The mayor's office is next door, and if he stands in just the wrong place, I can hear every word of his conversation. It's annoying."

"I know exactly what you mean," Sloth said, her mouth scrunching up in a sad little twist. "It happens to me *all* the time."

Pam cocked her head to the side, eyeing Sloth quizzically. I think she was about to ask what Sloth was talking about when the office door opened. An older, broad-shouldered man dressed impeccably in a charcoal suit strode into the office. He was swarthy, with white hair that glowed like a halo around a handsome, creased face. He was clearly elderly, maybe in his 70s, but he radiated vitality. I could tell just from looking at him he was a politician. And I could tell from the way Pam looked at him that this was the mayor.

"I was standing in the danger zone again, I know," he said, holding his hands up like he was under arrest. "I was ordering my wife's birthday present."

"You ordered *two* of whatever you purchased," Pam said, her brow arched. "How many wives do you have?"

"I bought her Baccarat candleholders," he said, laughing. "I couldn't get her just the one."

Pam raised a hand to her mouth, smothering a smile. "Julian, you do realize candlesticks are sold as a pair, right? You might want to check your credit card statement. Baccarat? I have a feeling you just spent a small fortune."

Julian blanched, his whole body freezing as he mentally tallied the amount of money he'd just accidentally spent. But then he laughed as he recovered, dusting his hands together and shaking his head playfully. "Well, that's why we pay you the big bucks, Pam. We can't all be beauty *and* brains." He flashed her a bright smile and looked around the room as though suddenly realizing he and Pam weren't alone. "My apologies, I didn't realize you had guests. I hope I'm not interrupting anything."

I had been enjoying their banter until that point, but with those words, I deflated. I hated it when people said things like that. Obviously, he was interrupting something. When people say things like that, the implication is that whatever they interrupted wasn't important. But whatever. He was a politician. It was his job to say meaningless words.

"I've just been giving the newest members of our community a history lesson," Pam said with a smile. "Mayor, these young people are from that reality TV show *Sinful House.* You remember the one. Finding the right location was all Portia talked about for months." She spoke Portia's name like the syllables might be poison. "This is Envy, this is Sloth, and this here is Pride. And this," she said, gesturing toward the mayor, "is Mayor Julian Gillespie."

The mayor went around the circle, shaking everyone's hand in turn. When my fingers closed around his hand, a lightning bolt shot down my spine. Images flashed before my eyes—a camping trip, a fishing expedition on a small boat, drinks by a fireplace. And in each of these visions, I saw the same face.

Edgar Thornton's face.

"My condolences for your loss," I said, not realizing I would say the words until they were already out of my mouth. The mayor's expression darkened, and I hurried to explain. "Sometimes, when I touch people, I see things. I saw you and Edgar fishing. You must have been close."

The mayor stared at me, his face blank. But his befuddlement lasted only a moment. He composed himself quickly, squaring his shoulders and dropping his chin to his chest as his politician's instincts kicked in. "Thank you. Edgar and I were close indeed. He was a good friend all the way from childhood, and I am devastated to have lost him." He looked to Pam. "In fact, if I believed in such a thing, I might say we should be on the lookout for more ill fortune. Within a short amount of time, I lost my best friend, and Pam here lost her sister. That's two tragedies. These things always come in threes."

The mention of ill fortune brought the Star of the Sea to mind, and my mouth went dry as I recalled the statue's posture, the way she held her face as she screamed. It was just a coincidence, though, wasn't it? Two deaths that touched the mayor's office had nothing to do with the statue's appearance on our lawn.

Still, I couldn't shake Greed's words: "An unexpected visitor will bring disaster and bad luck."

I shuddered and looked away.

Envy adjusted in her seat, leaning forward and

touching Pam lightly on the arm. "I'm so sorry about your sister, as well."

"Oh, they weren't close," Sloth interjected. As soon as she said it, she covered her mouth and blushed bright red as she turned to Pam. "I mean…you were estranged, weren't you?"

Pam gawped, lips twitching as her mouth fell open. Her gaze fluttered to the mayor, who offered only a bewildered lift of his shoulders in response. "I'm sorry," the woman stammered, blinking quickly, "but why would you say that? Did you know Fiona?"

Sloth waved both hands in front of her face, her cheeks growing impossibly redder. "No, I…oh, geez, I'm sorry. It was an accident. I didn't mean to see it. It was just right *there*," she explained, making a plucking motion by her forehead. She looked over to me, her expression harried and desperate.

It took me a second to realize she meant she'd accidentally read Pam's thoughts.

I made a patting motion at Sloth, and she settled down, though she reached for a pigtail and began chewing on it with a vengeance. I gave Pam what I hoped was a reassuring smile. "Sloth is a mind-reader. Don't worry; she's very ethical. She really tries not to look at other people's thoughts. But I guess she couldn't help but see that you and your sister weren't close."

Still visibly flustered, Pam re-crossed her legs and settled back into her seat, eyeing Sloth warily. "I see. Well, you're right, my sister and I were estranged. It was a stupid disagreement over *property* of all things. She owned a bit of land downtown that I rented from her. I wanted to buy it, but she wasn't interested in a sale."

"Was that before she got sick?" Envy asked. "I mean, she had Alzheimer's, right? That's what Danielle Martin told us."

Pam sat motionless a long moment before answering. "No," she said finally. "It wasn't dementia. She developed a condition called *atypical alogia*." She spoke the words with clinical detachment like a doctor delivering a poor prognosis to a bereft family. "She was incapable of speaking much at a time; no more than a few sentences, and that was considered a lot. And when she did speak, she could only recite things she'd read. Her mind grabbed onto written words like a vice, and she could parrot them back. But she couldn't produce her own thoughts."

"That's so sad," Envy said. "I'm sorry."

Pam tried on a smile, but it didn't quite reach her eyes. "It's all right. As I've said, we weren't close."

"I'm not close to my sister, either," Sloth said, her eyes downcast. "I'm sort of the black sheep of the family, I guess. Hadley—that's my sister—she's everyone's favorite. When we were kids, I worshiped her. She's the oldest. I wanted to be just like her."

Pam nodded. "Fiona was a year older than me," she said, a hint of sadness underlying her words. "So I understand."

"It's strange how sibling rivalries work," Sloth continued. "All I ever did was idolize Hadley. So it never made any sense why she hated me so much."

The room fell quiet, and we all averted our eyes. I

didn't have any siblings, so I couldn't relate to this. But based on my admittedly thin knowledge of human nature, it rang true. People hated each other for no reason all the time. You just had to read social media for five minutes to see that.

"Well, I don't want to keep you," the mayor said suddenly, clapping his hands together to break the uncomfortable silence. "When you finish your visit, Pam, would you mind coming to my office? I'd like to go over the proposed Bozeman budget for next week's meeting."

Pam nodded distractedly, and the mayor bid the rest of us a polite farewell before disappearing out the door. When he was gone, Pam cleared her throat and ran a hand gently over her hair, smoothing it back. "I apologize for that disruption," she said. "But it seems the mayor needs me, so I really need to get back to work. Was there anything else you wanted to know?"

"I think that's everything," Sloth said, climbing to her feet. Pamela returned the map, and Sloth tucked it carefully away. "You've been so helpful. We would never have figured out the arches on our own. Who knew there used to be a mission here in Odyssey?"

"Few people, I assure you," Pam said with a chuckle. "Odyssey has grown so rapidly that most of our citizens are transplants. Few of us have been here for generations, and even the older families probably forgot about the museum." Pam guided us to the door, her hands folded neatly before her. "Well, if you think of anything else, don't hesitate to get in touch. I am always happy to speak to our constituents."

As we filed out the door, I could just make out the mayor's voice drifting from his office. "Yes, I heard about Portia Cameron running against me. Her candidacy is a *joke*. That woman must have mounds of skeletons that will tumble from her closet the minute my people start to poke around. At least one of her associates has already been to jail!" He paused. "No, come on, Harlan, I wouldn't stoop so low as to ask Karen McMurtry anything—I don't care how good her information is. Besides, unless you've got a Ouija Board, that's a no-go. Didn't you hear? She passed away."

The door behind us clicked closed, and Pam Arquette breezed into the hall, leaving behind the smell of lilac perfume. "I just thought of something," she said. "You should come to the Coldwater silent art auction. We're trying to fund a much-needed performing arts center out on the outskirts of town. Lower property taxes," she added with a wink. "It's coming up soon— I'll put your names on the invite list. Bring your camera man. It'll be great fun." She gave a little finger wave and then hurried into the mayor's office.

Envy looked at me, her nose scrunched. "I think I'll be busy washing my hair that night," she said.

I chuckled. "I think we'll *all* be busy washing our hair that night."

"Not me," Sloth said. "Sounds like fun. Besides, my hair hardly ever needs that much washing."

To her credit, Envy physically bit her lip instead of responding to this as we headed back to the car.

eight

· · ·

When we arrived home, I made a beeline for the kitchen, visions of fried chicken and tacos with mango salsa dancing in my head. It was almost time for 'family dinner,' and if there was one thing I loved about Sinful House, it was Gluttony's cooking. Nothing got me out of bed faster than the smell of his homemade biscuits and gravy or peach-pecan buttermilk waffles. Even thinking about his food made my mouth water.

But to my utter heartbreak, I found the kitchen empty. Nothing was on the stove, and the countertops were bare. My stomach growled in response, and I patted my belly absently. It wasn't like Gluttony to forget dinner, so I went to go find him.

I didn't have to look long. I found him upstairs, huffing and puffing as he dragged a mattress down the hallway. Beads of sweat popped out along his brow, and his t-shirt was damp.

"Uh, Gluttony? What are you doing?" I asked. "Not

to be an ungrateful jerk, but there's no dinner in the kitchen. Are we not eating together tonight?"

Gluttony frowned and shooed me aside as he tugged the mattress over the carpet. Not wanting to look like a complete twit, I grabbed the front of the mattress and pulled. "Where are we taking this?"

"Here," he grunted, turning into Envy's bedroom. Inside, he leaned the mattress against a wall. "Can't you see I'm busy? If you're hungry, there are leftovers from yesterday. I ain't your mama, and you ain't helpless. Go heat something up and leave me be."

I glanced around the room, my face twisted in a frown. "What's going on here? These aren't even Envy's things. Where's all Envy's stuff?"

Gluttony tilted his head toward the hallway. "Ask Greed about it. I'm just doing what I'm told."

I left Envy's room and found Greed down the hallway in his own room. He was standing in a corner, arms folded over his chest, wearing an expression I couldn't read. The room was a wreck, and that wasn't like Greed, who was meticulous. But then I realized that wasn't the only thing different. The room was a tangle of furniture, books, trinkets, and clothes—Envy's clothes.

"Greed?" I gestured around at the mess. "What the heck is going on here?"

Before Greed could answer, Envy popped out of the closet, a huge smile on her face. "Have you seen this closet?" she asked. "It's like twice the size of my old one. Look at this." She bounced over to the large set of windows that made up most of the western wall and spread her arms wide, indicating the view of the beach. "Remember when we first moved in, and I was *so* sad because my room faced east? Well, Greed's room faces west, and he's agreed to switch with me. That's why he called me earlier." She squealed, hopping up and down with excitement. "This is like, the best day of my life."

Greed was still standing quietly in the corner. He wasn't smiling. His gaze was soft and distant, and his lips twitched just a little. If I had to guess, I'd say he looked pensive, but my knowledge of Greed's expressions was minuscule. "Greed? You're switching rooms with Envy? Why?"

Lust sauntered into the room then, her hair falling in long, loose waves over her shoulders. As soon as I saw her, my heart skipped a beat. Man, she looked great. She was wearing a bright red midriff with white capri pants that showed off her curves. Her feet were bare, and her toes were painted bright red to match her shirt. I was halfway in love with her all over again before I scolded myself to get it together. Whatever I thought was happening between me and Lust was a figment of my imagination. I'd seen the way she'd snuggled up to Greed when our new assignments were handed out. She wasn't into me, she was just flirty. I couldn't forget that.

But it sure was rough.

"Greed had another premonition," Lust said, her voice all sultry and velvety. "It happened today while we were driving around town." She paused, glancing over at Greed. It was only now that I realized their expressions matched. They looked somber.

My stomach did a little flip. Something was wrong.

"What did you see?" I asked.

Greed was quiet for a long stretch, and with each word he didn't speak, my anxiety grew, inching up my spine. "Greed? Hello? What's going on? What was your premonition about?"

"You," he said simply, not looking in my direction. "And Envy. I saw you and Envy in a room full of fire."

The room fell silent. Envy stepped away from the window, coming nearer to Greed, but stopped at a heap of clothing on the floor. "What? You didn't say anything. Why didn't you tell me?"

"I'm telling you now," he said. "I don't mean to be glib. I was waiting for the right time, but the feeling is starting to fade, so it's now or never. I saw you and Pride in a dark room with flames licking up the walls. I smelled smoke. I heard screaming." He let his gaze fall on Envy. "I saw flames reflected in your eyes. And though I can't be sure," he drawled, "I think I saw one of your elementals. A being made entirely of fire."

Envy blanched, covering her mouth with both her hands. Ever since she'd arrived at Sinful House, Envy had been accidentally—well, sometimes on purpose— summoning elementals to help around the house. First, she summoned a water elemental to keep the house clean. That ended in disaster for Sloth, who found all her things drowning in the undine's continual deluge. Next, Envy tried to rid our house of negative energy by letting her air elemental cleanse the place with smoke. Of course, the elemental went crazy and the entire house was so smoke-filled, one of our neighbors called the fire department. Our furniture would smell like patchouli for weeks. And then, most recently, she summoned an earth elemental to help with the grocery shopping. She lost control of him too, and the gnome threw a tantrum, throwing bread everywhere until local blabbermouth Stephanie Jones called security and got us in trouble with the network.

Envy's track record with elementals was not great, to say the least.

I turned to Greed, hands held out before me. "I'm not following," I said. "What does this have to do with switching rooms with Envy?"

Greed chuckled darkly, his chin falling to his chest as he smiled. "Envy has wanted this room since the beginning. A quick Google search shows that having a bedroom in the western part of the home imparts a healing spirit to the room's inhabitants. I suspect that if her temperament is more balanced and her thinking clearer, she might be less apt to accidentally summon elementals she can't control. A fire elemental is dangerous enough. Coupled with the bad luck the Star of the Sea brings?" He sighed morosely. "I may be your competitor, but that doesn't mean I want you to *die*."

My thoughts drifted to something the mayor said earlier, and I muttered, "Tragedy always comes in threes."

As soon as I said this, Gluttony stormed into the room, his nostrils flared. "All right," he growled. "I've had enough of this talk about bad luck. I don't know what that statue in our yard is supposed to mean, if it means anything at all. All this doomsday talk about bad luck ends now. I want all of you to meet me downstairs in ten minutes."

Envy looked over her shoulder at the mess that was her new room. "Uh, but we're not fini—"

"*Ten minutes*," Gluttony growled again before stomping out of the room.

I listened for the sound of footsteps retreating downstairs. Then I shrugged. "You heard the man. Ten minutes."

Leaving Greed and Envy to finish their swap, I went back to my room and shut the door. Just as I was taking off my shoes and eyeing my favorite pair of Star Wars pajamas, my phone buzzed atop my desk.

Except it wasn't my phone. It was Edgar Thornton's phone. Envy must have put it in my room so it didn't get lost in the move.

I hesitated, unsure of the protocol for answering a dead man's phone. But when I saw who the call was from, I picked up. "Edgar Thornton's phone," I said.

The line was silent for a beat. Then, Danielle said, "Is that you, Pride?"

"It is. Danielle, why are you calling me on this phone?"

Danielle sighed heavily into the receiver. "I could ask the same question. I said you could reach me anytime, and that my number was in my father's phone. But I didn't expect you would actually call me from my father's number. Do you know how disconcerting it is to see a missed call from your late father? You almost gave my poor mother a heart attack."

I groaned as a flush crawled into my cheeks. She was

right. That was idiotic of us. "I can only imagine," I agreed. It was as close to an apology as I could get. "It won't happen again. Listen, we called to ask you a question."

"All right. Whatever you need," Danielle said.

"We need to know who else knew about the talking corpses. Besides you, your brother, and your father."

For a moment, Danielle said nothing. "Well, it was a secret," she said at last. "We didn't want anyone to know."

"That doesn't answer my question. Look, this is important. It might be a clue in your father's murder."

Danielle was quiet a moment. When she spoke again, her voice was breathy. "Why are you asking questions about my father's murder? Are you working with the police?"

"Yes," I answered. "Sort of. Can you just answer me? Who else knew?"

I heard Danielle take a sharp breath on the other end. "Well…I don't know what use it could possibly be to you, but the only person I told was my realtor. I needed to know if a haunting would affect our property value," she explained.

My mouth went dry and my palms filmed over with sweat. "Danielle, your realtor wouldn't be Portia Cameron, would it?"

Danielle hesitated. "Yes, that's right. Why?"

"No reason," I said, my thoughts racing. "Hey, did you happen to tell her what the corpses said?"

"No, I didn't. Why do you ask?"

My thoughts were going a thousand miles a minute,

and I wasn't ready to verbalize anything yet, so I said, "I'm just trying to piece together who knows what. Listen, I gotta go, Danielle. I'll talk to you later."

I hung up the phone, my thoughts drifting back to my visit at City Hall. What had Mayor Gillespie said about Portia's campaign? Something about a host of skeletons falling out of her closet once anyone started to look? He was probably right about that. As a mayoral candidate, Portia might have motive to silence the likes of Karen McMurtry, especially if she didn't know all the corpses just spewed indecipherable nonsense.

But I didn't have time to think about that in any detail. I needed to meet Gluttony and the rest of the house downstairs.

———

The kitchen table set with seven bowls of caramel popcorn—one for each housemate. The camera crew was already waiting for us, lined up against the wall, cameras rolling, their red lights blinking annoyingly. I sat at my usual place and waited for the rest of the house to appear. When we were all present, Gluttony folded his hands over his ample stomach and leaned back, his eyes narrowing as he studied each of us. "Ever since that statue appeared, y'all have been acting like we're doomed," he said, his voice grave. "Wrath and Greed made a huge mess in our front yard—and I'd like to point out that you haven't filled in that hole you made. I suggest you get to that. We don't need the HOA harassing us about it."

"Oh, they've already been harassing the network," Sloth chimed in helpfully. "The president of the HOA called Tricia directly. Tricia promised to send a landscape crew to fix anything we messed up."

"That's what we should have done in the first place," Wrath scowled. "Called a crew to remove the statue. I mean, look at these hands, man." He held them up, twisting them this way and that. "Do these hands look like they know how to do manual labor?"

"I didn't ask you all here to talk about the HOA," Gluttony cut in, his voice booming over the others. "I want to talk about your attitudes. Listen. I don't know much, but I know one thing. Life is what you make of it. If you go looking for bad things, you will find them. Bad things are everywhere, statue or no statue. But I also know if you go looking for good things, you'll find that, too. So, I want y'all to eat this popcorn because it's delicious, and I made it myself. And then I want us to go around the table one by one and talk about something good that has happened since you've been at Sinful House."

If there was one thing I hated—well, it was shopping. But if there were two things I hated, the first was shopping, and the second was being forced into group activities. I wasn't in kindergarten. I didn't have to let Gluttony boss me around. But even though I wanted to object, Gluttony's heart was in the right place. And talking about good things that happened since we'd been at the house couldn't hurt.

I mean, I wasn't sure it would *help*, but whatever. The cameras were rolling, and cooperation would probably win me some votes. Plus, we had popcorn. I shoveled a handful into my mouth. It was sweet, buttery, sticky, and chewy, and I instantly felt refreshed when the sugar and salt hit my tongue.

"I'll go first," Envy said. "Since we've been at Sinful House together, I've gotten a brand-new bedroom that overlooks the ocean. Now I get to fall asleep listening to the waves crashing on the shore like I was destined to. I bet with all the amazing beauty rest, I'll get *so* many new Instagram followers."

"I'll go," Sloth said. "Since I've been at Sinful House, Gluttony has baked two dozen complimentary muffins just so I'd have a good day. That was really thoughtful of you," she said to Gluttony. "But that's not the only good thing that's happened. I also met a nice old woman who became my friend, and I cared for her quite a lot. Unfortunately, she ended up getting murdered."

Gluttony pounded the table, making our popcorn bowls quake. "Don't do that," he said. "I mean it. Good things only."

Sloth sucked in a breath. "You didn't let me finish. She got murdered, but we took her ghost to a really nice clubhouse for ghosts, and I think she's going to enjoy the rest of her afterlife there. The end."

When no one else immediately volunteered to go, I lowered my eyes and kept very still. I thought maybe if I didn't look at anyone, I'd become invisible, and I wouldn't have to play this absolutely mortifying game.

"I won last week's vote," Wrath said. "That's mine."

"And I signed a contract to publish a new article on personality disorders," Greed added.

"That's great, Greed. Congratulations," Gluttony said with a nod. "My sister had a baby. I'm an uncle."

Murmurs of congratulations went around the table before everyone went quiet. I felt my face burn hot. Had everyone gone? Was I the only one left? I held my breath and squeezed my eyes shut like a child who pretended if they couldn't see, they couldn't be seen.

Maybe I was still a kindergartener after all.

"Since I've been at Sinful House, I met someone who has become important to me. I've discovered that sometimes, your heart can take you for a wild ride."

I looked up to find Lust across the table, staring right at me. "I met Pride at Sinful House," she continued, "and that's made all the difference."

I was about one millisecond away from bursting into flames, so I dropped my gaze back into my lap, my palms practically dripping sweat. This was a plot twist I was not prepared for. What did she want from me? Was this an olive branch? Was this just Lust being Lust? Was she doing this for the viewers? I looked to Envy, hoping her expression might clue me in to how I should feel. But she was shoveling popcorn into her face, paying no attention to my absolute mortification.

"Pride," Greed said, "would you like to respond to Lust?"

Respond? To Lust? Right here in front of everyone? I would have sooner cut my finger off with a rusty pocket knife. But instead of saying that, I squeaked out, "I've enjoyed meeting you as well, Lust." Which was true, even though it left out the finer points of what meeting her made me feel.

"This is good," Gluttony said, his mouth also full of half-chewed kernels. "See, this is what I'm talking about. This is how a family is supposed to behave. It's your turn, Pride. What good things have happened since you've been here?"

"I don't want to do this," I admitted. "Not because nothing good has happened here, but what if…I don't know, what if talking about the good things jinxes it?" That wasn't the real reason I didn't want to talk about this, but I wasn't going to admit that in front of actual living humans. "It seems to me like shining a light on your blessings is asking the universe to snatch them away."

Gluttony scoffed, shaking his head. "That's not how the universe works. You don't jinx good things by talking about them. You make more good things happen. If you want something positive in your life, speak it into existence, Pride. If I learned nothing else from my mama, I learned that. The universe is always listening. Speak what you want into existence."

I scooped a handful of popcorn into my mouth just to buy some time. Finally, I said, "You know what I really want? I want things to be simple. I want things to make sense. I want people to say what they mean and mean what they say." I turned my gaze to Lust and stared at her until she pressed a napkin to her lips and looked away.

"I'll drink to that," Wrath said, tossing a kernel into

the air and catching it in his mouth. "Anybody want to join me for an after-popcorn cocktail?"

As we all pushed away from the table and the others followed Wrath to the recreation room, I followed Gluttony to the kitchen. Looking over my shoulder to ensure no one was listening, I asked, "So, what did you put in the popcorn this time?"

Gluttony raised an eyebrow. "The popcorn? What do you mean?"

"*You* know," I said. "So? What's in it?"

"Well, all right, I guess I can share my secrets with you. Didn't take you for a candy-maker, though. That caramel is made with butter, cream, sugar—"

"Hilarious," I interrupted. "That's not what I'm talking about. I'm onto you, Gluttony. You always put magic in our food when you think there's a problem. So what did you add this time?"

My housemate grunted, picking up a rag to wipe down the counters. "Don't worry about it, Pride."

"But I *am* worried about it," I pressed, "because I don't like surprises. I don't want to be forced to tell the truth, I don't want to get chatty with strangers, and I don't want to walk around telling people how beautiful they are! So what did you spike the popcorn with?"

Gluttony heaved a sigh and shook his head. "Well, if you have to know, I put good luck in it. Y'all are so worried about that statue outside, and since we can't seem to move it, I thought I'd counterbalance it with some good juju."

I frowned. "So does that mean you believe the statue is a bad omen, too?"

Gluttony shook his head. "No. But y'all do. Beliefs matter, Pride. Your brain creates your reality. If you believe a thing, you manifest a thing. So go on, get out of my kitchen. Go enjoy your good luck." He winked and gestured toward the recreation room. "I'd start with Lust. She obviously has a thing for you."

"There's nothing obvious about Lust," I grumbled under my breath. "At least, not to me. But anyway, thank you. For the honesty and the good luck magic, I mean. Just…thanks."

I ambled out of the kitchen and trekked up the stairs to my room. I was feeling better already. With each step, I could literally feel my luck changing. Maybe Greed's weird feng shui would stop Envy from lighting us on fire, maybe it wouldn't. But with Gluttony's good luck magic coursing through my veins, I no longer had to worry about it.

For the first night in a while, I slept like a baby.

nine

. . .

"**Y**ou're crazy if you think I'm not coming with you."

Sloth and I were slipping on our shoes and heading out to Déjà Brew when Envy cornered us, hands on her hips and determination in her eyes. "We're partners, Pride. Remember?"

I pushed around her, reaching for the door. "It's not a good idea, Envy," I said. "Sloth and I just need to take care of something really fast, and then you and I can go back to working the talking corpses case later today."

But Envy was not dissuaded. She elbowed me aside and planted herself in front of me, one hand on each side of the doorjamb, blocking my path. "You're not leaving this house without me," she said. "I need excitement, Pride. I'm so tired of watching everyone else's life on social media. My baby cousin got married last weekend, and you know how my love life is? I haven't had a date in six months! My other friends are climbing the corporate ladder and progressing their careers, and I'm still stuck in the same teaching position I've had for the past 10 years. And I love teaching. But I want something exciting to show for my life, too. It's not fair for everyone else to have all the fun. So if you think you're getting out of this house without me, you've got another think coming." She paused. "Do you want to take it right now?"

I growled. "Take *what* right now?"

"Your other *think*," she said with a grin. "You have one coming, after all."

I sighed and turned to Sloth, looking for help. But Sloth just shrugged and gestured with her chin toward the car. "If she wants to come, I say we let her. Three heads are better than two and everything."

I didn't think that was true, but it looked like I was outnumbered. With a dejected sigh, I nodded wearily. "Fine. Just let me and Sloth do all the talking, okay? And when we get there, don't touch anything. And whatever you do, don't *summon* anything."

Hands still planted in the doorway, Envy glowered at me and rolled her eyes. "*Obviously* I wouldn't summon anything. *Obviously* I'll be on my best behavior." Then she clapped her hands in excitement, bouncing on her toes as she squealed. "Oh my gosh, I've never been to a haunted café before! This is going to be the best day of my life."

As we headed for the car, I heard the soft whir of a spinning motor followed by a quick slurp. I turned around to see Beefy Camera Guy with his bag slung over a shoulder, drinking what looked like green sludge from a personal blender.

"Oh no, not you," I said, holding up a hand. "This is personal business. You're not invited."

"I'm real sorry, but the network says I've been too lenient with you," he said, licking a smear of green smoothie from the corner of his mouth. "They'll give me my walking papers if I don't tag along everywhere you go today. I've got a wife at home and a new baby on the way. I can't lose this job."

I did feel a twang of guilt at that, but there was no way I was letting the camera guy tag along. I didn't even want to get Envy involved. "Listen, this is my call, and I'm not taking 'The network said so' for an answer. I may have signed a contract, but I still have a personal life. Don't make this weird."

The camera guy laughed and gave me a genial clap on the arm. "Can it *get* any weirder?" he asked. "This is the weirdest job I've ever taken, and I worked on the set of *Dating Bigfoot*."

"And if you want to live to shoot *Marrying Bigfoot*, you'll go back inside and pretend you never saw us."

He huffed, huge shoulders sagging. "Fine. Have it your way, boss. But don't be surprised if your numbers go down this week. Again."

I said nothing to that, but I brooded over my tanking popularity all the way to Old Downtown. When we arrived at Déjà Brew, we had to stand in line for nearly 10 minutes as only one barista was working. Thankfully, that barista was Felix. As soon as he saw me, however, his expression darkened. "Can I get you something?" he asked, eyes darting nervously around the room.

"You definitely seem capable," I said, trying on my

best movie-star smile, which, let's be honest, was C-list level at best. "We were just headed downstairs. I assume that's okay?"

Felix folded his arms across his chest and shook his head. "Afraid not. New rules. The Crypt is off-limits until further notice."

I blinked. That was a predicament I didn't see coming. "Off-limits? Why?"

"I've been having trouble with one of the ghosts," Felix explained. "Somebody has been sneaking up the stairs and scaring the bejeezus out of my customers."

I quirked an eyebrow. "How? What's the ghost doing?"

"Shouting," Felix said with a sigh. "First it was pieces of poetry. Then it was corny jokes like you'd find on popsicle sticks. Most recently, it was recipes. The upside is, now I know how to make potatoes au gratin." Felix chuckled, shaking his head. "Anyway, I figured if we keep the door closed, the ghost can't sneak up here. So for now, no one goes into the Crypt."

I furrowed my brow in frustration. "Well…why don't you just ask the ghost to quit?"

"I tried that," Felix said. "But it didn't work. And it doesn't help that I can't see the culprit."

I frowned, tilting my head to the side in thought. "Wait a second. You can't see this ghost? It's invisible?"

"Appears so."

Sloth elbowed me playfully in the side. "Appears so. Get it? But it's invisible?"

"But you can hear it?" I asked, ignoring her. "And the *customers* can hear it?" That was the strangest news of all. Most people could neither see nor hear ghosts unless they were whisperers like me and Felix.

"That's right. Anyway, you can appreciate that I didn't want a ghost running around shouting recipes at my customers. So until I have time to figure that all out, nobody goes downstairs."

I ran my fingers through my hair. "Okay, but Felix… ghosts can go through walls."

"I know that," he grumbled. "But I'm hoping if I don't disturb them, they won't disturb me. The woman who owns this property was in here about a month or two ago. She's thinking of selling to a developer—condos, you know? She was real nice about it—said she'd give me a cash for the trouble of moving the store. So the last thing I need is for ghosts to mess that up for me."

"They're gonna turn Déjà Brew into condos?" I wrinkled my nose in distaste. "But this place is historic! Didn't there used to be a mission here or something?"

Felix shrugged. "I don't know. Maybe."

"Well, what about the ghosts?" I asked, my mind still turning. "Where will they go?"

"Yeah, that's a concern," Felix agreed. "Also, the Society will have to find somewhere else to operate. There's a lot of moving parts. Now, can I get you anything?"

Sloth sauntered up to the counter, chewing idly on the end of one of her pigtails. "Actually, can I get a double espresso?" As if underscoring her needs, she stretched her arms overhead, yawning noisily. "These early mornings are for the birds."

Felix quirked an eyebrow. "It's 10 a.m.," he said.

Sloth dug her knuckles into an eye socket and rubbed sleepily. "Yeah, that's what I mean. Better make that a triple. It's for Sloth."

The three of us found an empty table and slid into our chairs. When we were sure Felix wasn't paying us any attention, Envy leaned forward and whispered, "So, you know what we have to do, right?"

I raised an eyebrow. "What's that?"

A slow smile curled over her lips. "We'll have to come back here tonight when the place is closed and sneak in."

Sloth raised an eyebrow. "Sneak in? You mean *break* in."

I held my hands out in front of me, palms out as I shook my head. "Hold your horses there, Catwoman. We're not breaking into anywhere. No chance. Going to jail isn't part of my contract."

"There's a new moon tonight," Envy continued as though I hadn't spoken. "That means it'll be dark. We'll come down here late—maybe around two, three in the morning. We'll sneak into the café and go downstairs and investigate. It shouldn't take long, right? An hour, tops? We'll be out of here long before the commuter crowd even wakes up."

"Envy," I said, my voice sounding strained even to my ears, "this isn't a game. This is real life. You can't just break into someone's business. It's wrong on so many levels!"

"Well, we have to investigate that map," she pressed on. "What's down there? Why is there a star in the spot where Déjà Brew is today? People are *dead*, Pride. And this map is our best clue why."

"Yes!" I threw my hands up in exasperation. "Exactly! People are dead! That should be a starred reason in the Why We're Not Doing This Column, Envy!"

"Well, it's not," she retorted. "People have gotten killed over this, and the three of us are the only ones looking into it. But hey. If you don't want to go?" She gave a carefree shrug and turned her attention to Sloth. "You'll do this with me, won't you?"

Sloth traced a finger lazily over the table, making designs in the sugar someone had spilled. "Me? Yeah, I guess so. Sure, I'm in."

Envy gave a crisp nod and sat back in her seat, a smug smile playing over her lips. "So then it's settled. Sloth and I are on the case. Pride, you can stay home and watch TV or paint your nails with all the other girls."

I knew she was trying to goad me. This was, like, Reverse Psychology 101. I wasn't going to fall for it. I wasn't. I *wasn't.*

I turned to Sloth and gave her my best look of reproach. "You know this isn't a good idea," I said. "Come on, Sloth. This is nuts."

"Yeah, it kind of is," Sloth agreed, "but Envy's right. We haven't come this far to give up now. At least, I haven't. So if you want to sit this one out, that's fine. But I'm with Envy. Besides." She offered me a reproachful look of her own. "You didn't think you could peer pressure me into being a weenie, did you?"

Busted. I absolutely thought I could do that. I should have known better—Sloth looked harmless, but she was actually pretty hardcore underneath her jelly-stained pajamas. "Fine." I blew out my cheeks in defeat and leaned back in my seat. "Let's say I go along with this. Do you even know how to break into a building?"

"Not exactly," Envy admitted. "But look at the front door. It uses one of those electric keypads. And I just bet we know someone who'd make quick work of locks like that."

"Absolutely not," I objected, banging my hand on the table. The silverware rattled in response, and the table next to ours shot me a dirty look. I lowered my voice and jabbed a finger at Envy's chest. "Seriously, Envy. *No.* We're not dragging Wrath into this."

"To be fair," Sloth drawled, sticking a sugar-laden finger into her mouth, "Wrath is already involved. He knows about Chenoweth and the laptop. He's as involved as anyone."

"Then let me be honest," I said. "I don't want to work with the guy. *Again.* I just got rid of him! I don't know if you've noticed, but he's kind of a lot to handle, you know?"

Envy smirked. "I don't know if *you've* noticed, but so are you."

If you want to bruise a person's ego, let it slip that they're just as annoying as the person they're complaining about. It works every time. My pride wanted to object to Envy's well-placed but entirely unnecessary barb, but what could I say? I knew I was difficult. I had trouble with social situations. I rarely understood nuance or figurative language, and dealing with people sometimes made me want to stab myself with a fork. (That's not figurative language. I do sometimes *want* to stab myself in the thigh when people try to make small talk with me. But I don't because I have what Dr. Xena calls *impulse control.* And that's the difference between *wanting* to text your ex in the middle of the night but not actually *doing* it. Not that I have any experience with that kind of thing.)

But even with my flaws, I wasn't the one running around preaching the evils of capitalism and telling anybody who would listen that patriarchy and white supremacy were ruining Western society! I was the lesser of two evils! Surely my housemates could see that.

Right?

"Whatever," I said, soothing my battered ego by sniffing importantly and refusing to make eye contact. "I'm sure there will be nothing obvious about four people trying to break into a building after dark. This plan gets better and better by the second."

"I agree," Envy said, turning my sarcasm against me. "Just think about it, Pride. When it's all said and done, this will make for such an awesome story on TikTok."

"Triple espresso for Sloth?"

Sloth got up as her name was called and walked over to the counter to retrieve her coffee. When we were alone, Envy started picking at her nails and said casually, "You know what your problem is?"

"Yes," I sighed. "I suffer from a mix of social anxiety disorder and—"

"Your problem is you've played it safe your whole life," she interrupted. "Your parents vanished off the face of the earth when you were a baby. Your whole background is a mystery. I get that. Maybe if my whole life was overshadowed by some freak incident, I'd be more like you. But life is risk versus reward. If you never risk anything, you never get anything, either."

"I'll keep that in mind," I muttered, knowing I wouldn't. "Anyway, to change the subject, I finally got in touch with Danielle."

"So what did she say? Did she tell anybody about the talking corpses?"

I nodded. "You were right. She couldn't keep that secret to herself. She claims she only told one person. But guess who that one person was?"

Envy's eyes were bright with excitement as she shook her head. "I have no idea! Tell me."

I smiled. "Portia Cameron."

Envy blinked. "Who?"

Sloth returned just then, sliding into her seat as she slurped her espresso. "The woman who just announced she's running for mayor," Sloth put in. "Remember? Mayor Gillespie was shouting about it."

Envy snapped her fingers, eyes going wide. "Right! Now I see why you look so smug. Suppose Karen McMurtry had something on Portia, and Portia knew about the chatty corpses. In that case, she might worry that her secret wasn't, you know—taken to the grave, as they say."

I nodded, my brow furrowed in thought. "I know.

But it's still kind of a weak motive. We all have secrets we don't want getting out."

"But we're not all running for office," Sloth said.

"And as much as I dislike Portia," I continued, "and I really dislike her, like, a lot—I'm having a hard time seeing her as a murderer. I mean, shooting an old guy in cold blood?"

"Well, how well do you really know her?" Envy asked. "People have murdered for less. You can't assume what people are capable of just by having a passing acquaintance with them, right?"

I grunted. "I guess that's true."

"So have you shared this with Detective Doyle yet?"

I shook my head, drumming my fingers on the table. "No. I don't know how to relay the information in a way that makes sense. I mean, you and I know Portia has motive. But the detective doesn't know about the talking corpses and almost certainly wouldn't believe us even if we told him. So how can we make this make sense?"

Envy pressed her lips together and scooted to the edge of her seat, giving me a pointed look. "You're over-thinking this. Just tell the detective you got some evidence suggesting Edgar Thornton may have known a secret Portia didn't want to get out. You don't have to tell him Edgar heard the secret from a dead body."

I hated to admit it, but Envy was making sense. "Yeah, you're right. Let me give him a call."

I pulled out my phone and dialed.

"Doyle."

I cleared my throat and took a deep breath. "Hi, Detective. This is Pride. I have some information on the

Edgar Thornton case to share with you." I glanced at Envy, who made encouraging motions with her hands. "Well, we've been talking to some people around town, and it seems Edgar might have stumbled upon a secret about Portia Cameron she didn't want getting out."

The detective grunted. "We all have secrets we don't want getting out," he said.

I turned to my housemates and made a *See? That's what I said!* face, but they couldn't hear the other side of the conversation, so it had little effect. Into the phone, I said, "Right, but Portia just announced she's running for mayor next term. And if there's one thing I know about Portia Cameron, she's cutthroat. She's not much interested in losing."

The detective barked out a laugh. "You know I was married to her, right? I think I have a pretty good bead on her myself. So. You called to tell me I need to look into my ex-wife as a suspect. Well, isn't that rich? She digs her nose into my business and gives you the green light to investigate my case, and here you are telling me she's got motive. Well, sometimes life just hands you good news on a platter, doesn't it? Any idea what the secret was?"

"If I knew that," I drawled, "it wouldn't be a secret."

"Don't get smart," the detective growled. "I was just beginning to like you."

That was a lie, but I let it slide. "Quid pro quo, detective. Did your people find anything interesting at the crime scene?"

"Honestly, not much," the detective admitted with a weary sigh. "The scene was pretty clean. The only unusual thing we found was a used fogger. You know, the stuff you use to bomb the house when you have a bug infestation. Seems the mortuary must've been crawling with cockroaches."

That imagery was something straight out of a horror movie, and I shuddered violently. "You found that in the preparation room?"

"Yep. Well, we assume it's a bug bomb. Not familiar with the brand. The label just said 'CI'. Is there anything else?"

"No, that's everything," I said absently. I was still mulling over the can of bug poison left behind. Sure, a mortuary could have a bug problem just like anywhere else. But the preparation room? The immaculate room where morticians prepared the dead for viewing? It wasn't like you munched on chips and sandwiches in that room. So why would it have a bug problem?

"Well, I appreciate the tip on Portia," the detective said. He didn't really sound appreciative. "I'm sure nothing will come of it. As much as I'd like to hang this on my ex-wife, I'm not sure she's really the murdering type."

"It's not your job to guess," I said. "It's your job to uncover facts."

The detective scoffed into the receiver. "Right. Well, I can't say it's been a pleasure."

The line went dead.

I turned to Envy and Sloth and shrugged lamely. "They didn't find anything at the crime scene. Just a used canister of CI bug poison."

Sloth tapped her chin thoughtfully with a forefinger. "A canister of bug poison? Brand-name CI?"

I nodded. "That's what he said."

Sloth dug out her phone and tapped out a quick text message. "Hang on just a sec," she said, her face all squinched up as she typed. "I have a hunch, but I need Wrath's help."

A moment later, Sloth's phone pinged. She looked down to read the message, and her face lit up as she smiled with excitement. "Yep. That's what I thought. Here, Pride. Look at this."

Sloth handed me the phone, and I looked down to see a return text message from Wrath. He had attached a screenshot from a website I was now familiar with. It was the Chenoweth International website—specifically, their secret shopping page. The screenshot was of a product called MagicBloc™ Bomb. The canister looked just like a standard fogger, except the label was nondescript, bearing only the letters CI.

Of course. CI for Chenoweth International.

"It's a fogger, but it's not bug poison," I said, stating the obvious. "It's that MagicBloc stuff. Okay, wow. Now it all makes sense." I banged my forehead with the butt of my hand, aghast at my stupidity. "When I touched Edgar's corpse, nothing happened, remember? I should have felt something, especially after such a violent crime. I didn't, but now I know why. Somebody set off this fogger, dousing the whole room in MagicBloc, preventing my ability from firing." I looked at Sloth. "Chenoweth is the link. Edgar Thornton's murder and Eleanor Romanowsky's murder are related."

Envy grinned. "Still have cold feet about coming back here tonight?"

I shook my head. "Not anymore," I admitted. "There's too much at stake. Chenoweth has to be taken down."

ten

. . .

The four of us sneaked out of the house just after 2
a.m. Wrath took no convincing at all—in fact, he
was excited to do his part to "flip the tables on a fascist
organization." How he decided Chenoweth
International was fascist, I had no idea. But then again,
nothing about Wrath really made sense to me.

We parked the car two blocks from our destination
and walked the rest of the way. Just as Envy predicted,
the night was dark. The sliver of new moon gave off
little light as it played peekaboo with the clouds. Still, we
all wore dark colors to blend in with the night. I'd
donned a black hoodie and jeans with the hood pulled
tight around my face. We crept along Odyssey's streets
without speaking, keeping our hands in our pockets and
our heads ducked low.

As we neared Déjà Brew, we slowed our pace. Envy
nudged Wrath to the front of our line, where he moved
with quiet caution toward the door. He glanced over his

shoulder and then tried the door handle. "Locked," he said.

"Of course it's locked," Envy hissed impatiently. "It's 2 o'clock in the morning! That's why we brought you in the first place. Now hurry up and do your magic or whatever it is you do. We need to get off the street."

Wrath scowled and made a rude gesture at Envy but leaned forward toward the lock just the same. When he was eye level with it, he whispered, "Okay, open up you piece of—"

An electric whir and the metallic sound of something clicking was all we heard. When Wrath tried the doorknob again, the door slid soundlessly open.

"We're in," he grinned. Then he disappeared through the door, and the rest of us followed.

We paused inside Déjà Brew, getting our bearings and letting our eyes adjust to the dark. At night, everything looks sinister. My mind played tricks on me, convincing me I saw the shadowy profiles of the bad guys we were hunting waiting around every corner. Taking a deep inhale to steady my nerves, I motioned for my housemates to follow me as I led them to the back room and down the secret staircase that led into the Crypt.

At the bottom of the stairs, I flipped a switch, and dim, honey-colored light infiltrated the darkness. The ghosts were still milling around, looking unperturbed by our late-night arrival. Most of the ghosts sat around in little clusters, chatting with their friends or reading books. It was the reading part I found interesting. In all the years I'd been dealing with ghosts, I'd rarely seen them interact with physical objects. But several of these ghosts were doing just that, flipping through the pages of various tomes on topics such as cryptozoology, telekinesis, and UFOs. I wondered idly if ghosts could *learn* to touch things. I'd have to look into it later.

"So," Sloth said, interrupting my thoughts. "What exactly are we looking for?"

I surveyed the room, taking in the possibilities. The Crypt was filled with arcane books and paraphernalia, containing everything from Ouija boards to prints of sacred geometry. "I'm not sure, to be honest. All I know is this place is important to Chenoweth for some reason. Just look for weird stuff, I guess."

Sloth gestured around sleepily. "Yeah, okay, but this whole place is weird stuff, Pride."

I grunted. "I don't know what else to tell you. Just start searching."

The four of us split up, each taking a separate section of the room. Nobody spoke, but I felt the heaviness of our task hanging in the air. All we had to go on was a star on an old, crappy map. We could be looking for anything, and that thought was too depressing for words.

But then I remembered Gluttony and the magic he put in the popcorn. Good luck magic. So I took a breath and got to work.

As I was opening drawers and rooting through the contents, I heard a familiar voice behind me. "Hello again."

I turned around to found to find Angelica Muñoz floating behind me. She looked chipper, and I was glad to see her. "Hi yourself," I said, smiling. "How's death treating you?"

"I can't complain. There's no one around to listen." She glanced around the room at the rest of my house-mates. "What are you all doing here?"

I ran a hand through my hair and heaved a noisy sigh. "Well, we're looking for something, but we're not sure what. Something out of place or unusual. You live down here, so maybe you've seen something out of the ordinary?" I asked hopefully.

The ghost tapped a finger to her lips thoughtfully. "Well, it's just a basement. A very fancy basement, but still. Mostly it's just a place for ghosts to mingle and the Society to do...whatever it is they do. Which isn't much."

My rising optimism sank. "No? What *do* they do here?"

"They gossip," the ghost said with a roll of her eyes. "*So* much gossip. You would think these people had better things to do with their lives. But I guess they don't have to work for a living, so how else are they supposed to fill their time? You know what they say: Great minds discuss ideas. Average minds discuss events. Small minds discuss other people. And I assure you, the Society is filled with the smallest-minded people I've ever met."

I chuckled wryly. "What do they gossip about?"

Angelica sighed. "All kinds of things. Who's dating who, who's cheating on who, who lost money in the stock market, stuff like that. Honestly, it's like an endless episode of *Real Housewives of Odyssey, California.*" The ghost smiled and leaned her head to the side, thinking.

"Sometimes, they talk about city business. At least a handful of them are on the city council."

That piqued my interest. "Really? Who?"

"Well, let's see. There's this blonde woman. I think she's named after a car? Mercedes or Lexus or—"

"Portia?"

Angelica nodded. "That's it. Portia. You know her?"

"Yes," I stammered. "But…wait, she's a member of the *Society?* Are you sure? She hates the supernatural!"

Angelica shrugged. "Yeah, well, she acts like the leader of the crew. The *actual* leader is this woman Victoria, but Portia wears the pants in that relationship, if you know what I mean."

I was positive I'd seen both Portia and Victoria wear pants, so I wasn't sure why that was relevant. The ghost continued, "There's also this guy, Anthony. He's not so bad—easy on the eyes, anyway, if you know what I mean. And then there's his friend, Wilson. He's a giant nerd, and he *clearly* doesn't care about politics. Beats me why he sits on the council at all—he looks *so* bored any time they stop talking about hauntings or astral travel and start yammering about propositions and elections. And then there's this other woman, Natalie—she seems okay. Kind of a wallflower. But they all sit on the council together."

I whistled. "Four Society members are also on the council? That seems like a lot. How many council members does a city like Odyssey have, anyway?"

Angelica shrugged. "You're asking the wrong chick. Politics is not my bag. Anyway, I don't pay too much attention to what they do or what they talk about. I wouldn't have spent time around people like that in life, and I certainly try to avoid them in death."

I was opening my mouth to respond when I heard a sharp intake of breath and Envy saying, "Pride, come check this out."

I excused myself and drifted over to where Envy was peering into the pages of a spiral-bound notebook. Her brow was creased as she read. "What did you find?"

"You tell me." She pressed the notebook into my hands. "It looks like meeting minutes. Does any of this sound familiar to you?"

I looked down into the handwritten notes and began skimming the pages. It wasn't exactly riveting, just a bunch of mumbo-jumbo about dues, initiation ceremonies, fundraisers, and—

And then it hit me. These words *were* familiar.

I read aloud from the page. "Discussion, new location. Wilson proposes City Hall for new location if we can get a friend or colleague into office. WB will ask Pam to order blueprints of emergency shelter. Outstanding questions, what are the dimensions for the room? Discussion, birthday party ideas for WB. Notes, WB is allergic to chocolate."

I looked up and shut the book. "This is what we heard on Edgar Thornton's phone." I scrunched up my face in bewilderment. "The stupid corpses were relaying Paranormal Society meeting minutes? What for?"

Envy chewed on her bottom lip, shaking her head in equal dismay. "I don't know. There's got to be a connection between the Society and the deceased. Or maybe a connection between the Society and Edgar? Maybe he was a member?"

"Maybe," I agreed, handing the journal back to Envy. "Great find on the minutes, even if I don't know what it means yet. Hang onto those, okay? They might come in useful later."

Envy stuffed the notebook into her purse and I drifted away to continue looking around. The Paranormal Society had a lot of curious memorabilia. The walls were lined with paintings, strange photos, and even old lithographs. I was turning away from an aged gravestone rubbing when something about it caught my eye, and I doubled back.

I blinked, re-reading the words I had glossed over a moment before. I didn't speak Spanish, so I didn't know what they meant. But as I read the words aloud, a shiver ran down my spine.

"Magdalena. Ahora con los angeles, protegiéndonos desde arriba."

A voice at my side startled me. "Magdalena. That must be the medicine woman Pam told you about."

I looked over to find the ghost girl fidgeting beside me. Her face was upturned, and she stood on tiptoes to better see the rubbing. She pointed at the framed paper and scrunched up her face. "Can you get that down for me? It's too high to see."

"Since when are you interested in headstone inscriptions?" I asked, gently lifting the rubbing from its nail. "I thought you were only interested in random animal facts. Can you even read Spanish?"

"No," the ghost said, pressing herself close to peer at

the artwork. I kneeled low so she could get a better look. "But it's pretty, don't you think? How are these made?"

"You cover a headstone with a lightweight paper like vellum and then you gently rub over it with charcoal or a pencil until you've captured the engraving on the paper," I explained. "It's very tedious and time-consuming to do it well because you don't want to damage the headstone."

The ghost nodded. "It was worth it. Her headstone must have been beautiful. This flower looks like the California poppy," she said, pointing. "It's kind of hard to tell, though. But this is definitely a quail, the California state bird. Did you know the common quail can run almost 40 miles per hour?"

I was about to say that seemed impossible given their short legs when a voice behind me said, "It says, 'Now with the angels, protecting us from above.'"

Angelica moved next to me, too, until the three of us were huddled together over the grave rubbing. "Magdalena is one of the folk saints of Odyssey. Unofficially, of course. But it's said she looks over us. She guides us."

"Who's us?" I asked. "The people who live in Odyssey?"

"No," the ghost girl whispered somberly, her eyes wide and round. "The people who die in Odyssey." She looked around, a slow smile spreading on her cupid bow mouth. "There's power here," she said. "Don't you feel it?"

I opened my mouth to say I didn't feel anything when an image popped into my mind—handwritten words on a carefully hidden piece of paper that read

"Nexus of Power," accompanied by a star that marked the very location I was standing in now.

Goosebumps broke out along my skin, and the hairs at the back of my neck stood up. I rose to put the artwork back where I'd found it, but as I moved to place the frame on the nail, I stopped short.

An inch beneath the nail was a small, circular indentation in the wall. It almost blended in perfectly with the texture of the drywall, but it was faintly outlined.

It wasn't merely an indentation. It was a button.

"What the…?"

The ghost girl pressed herself against my legs. "What is it?"

"I don't know," I said, my words barely a whisper. I placed a forefinger against the button and, my lip folded beneath my teeth, pressed it.

A deep grumbling filled the Crypt, followed by shouts and squeals of surprise. Quickly, I placed Magdalena's grave rubbing back on the wall and backed away, my eyes searching the room for the source of the disruption.

"This can't be happening," Wrath breathed.

I followed Wrath's gaze, and my mouth fell open. On the other side of the room, a giant bookshelf had slid aside to reveal a corroded metal door bearing the same keypad lock as the front door to Déjà Brew.

"I think we found what we're looking for," Sloth said.

"Wrath?" I whispered. "Can you open that?"

Envy slipped her arm through mine, trembling at my side as we approached the door. Wrath pushed up his sleeves and took a deep breath. He leaned forward, whispered something to the lock, and the door beeped.

With my heart in my throat, I reached out, fingers closing around the doorknob. I turned, and the door creaked open.

eleven

. . .

"A secret passage?" Envy breathed, digging her fingers into my bicep. "Are you *kidding* me? Oh wow, this is the best day of my life. I had no idea when I woke up this morning I would be living in a Sherlock Holmes novel. Eat your heart out, Becca Daniels!"

"Who's Becca Daniels?" Sloth asked.

"Third-grade teacher," Envy answered. "She thinks she's hot stuff because she has 10,000 followers on Instagram. It's just because she likes to show off her—"

"Quiet." I brought a finger to my lips and disentangled from Envy as I stepped into the darkness. The hallway was cool and damp and smelled of algae, decay, and saltwater. Up ahead, the hallway met another hallway, forming an intersection. We appeared to be in some kind of tunnel network, connecting unfinished passages beneath Old Downtown. Everything around us was stone or concrete, and as soon as the door behind us closed, we were plunged into total darkness. Wrath pulled out his cellphone and activated its flashlight.

That's when we noticed this side of the door had no lock. And no handle for that matter.

"This has to be some kind of joke," Wrath said, cursing under his breath. "Are we trapped down here? Can we get back inside?"

Sloth placed a hand on Wrath's shoulder and squeezed. "We'll cross that bridge when we come to it," she said. "Come on. Let's find whatever we came down here to find."

She pushed Wrath forward with a comforting smile. But I saw the way her lips trembled when his back was turned.

Quietly, we padded down the corridor, hardly daring to breathe. At the first intersection, I looked both ways and then placed my right hand on the wall. "Right-hand turns only," I instructed. "As long as I keep contact with the wall, we should find a way out. I think," I amended under my breath.

"Where do you think we are?" Sloth whispered. Her voice echoed through the underground. "We're not underneath Déjà Brew anymore."

"Definitely not," Wrath said. "We seem to have stumbled into some kind of underground railroad. I had no idea something like this would exist in California."

"There are tunnels just like these underneath Los Angeles," I said, keeping my voice low and my hand on the wall as we walked. "They were originally used for streetcars, safer ways to transport money between banks, and finally for bootleggers. The tunnels are mostly unmapped, so they're not really safe to use. But they still exist today."

"I wonder if this tunnel system was part of the original mission," Envy mused. "Do you think anyone even knows they're here?"

"Someone knows," I said. "That's why the door we just went through was both hidden and locked. You wouldn't want anyone to sneak into your business via these tunnels. I assume Felix knows. And if he does, others do." I thought about Envy's equation about secrets. Old Downtown consisted of three different streets. If half the proprietors in the area knew about the tunnels…well, you do the math.

"Look," Sloth said, pointing. "A door."

We paused before an old door painted with chipped, faded green paint. It was coated with grime, rust, and spiderwebs. It evidently hadn't been used in a while, though it at least had a handle. Wrath stepped toward it, hands deep in the kangaroo pocket of his hoodie. "Should we try it?" he asked.

"No guts, no glory," Envy said, nodding.

Wrath reached for the handle and pulled. Unsurprisingly, the door didn't budge. It was locked from the other side. Wrath bent down and whispered the same way he'd done for the locks at Déjà Brew.

Nothing happened.

Frowning, Wrath stood up. "This one must be mechanical instead of electrical," he said. "I can't get us inside that one, man. Maybe we'll have better luck with the others."

A little further on, we came to another door. Just like the green door, this one was old and rusted. Wrath tried his technopathy again to no avail. We moved along, continuing to make right-hand turns and trying any doors we came across. So far, Gluttony's good luck wasn't exactly panning out.

"Here's another one," Wrath said, coming upon another ill-used door. He reached for the handle and pulled. Like the others, nothing happened. "This is getting old, man. I'm starting to get claustrophobic."

"You're the one who wanted to come," Envy reminded him.

"You're the one who asked me!" he hissed. "You think I was just jonesing to go spelunking in the middle of the night?"

"Just try to open the door," Sloth reprimanded, "and quit whining."

Wrath huffed out a sigh, ran his hands through his hair, and put his palms on the door. His voice trembled only slightly when he said, "Time to open up, old buddy, old pal."

To my surprise, a familiar whirring sound was followed by an electric click. We gasped collectively as Wrath's hand found the door handle and pulled.

The door swung open.

No one spoke as we entered the room. Like the tunnel, it was pitch black, illuminated only by the thin glow of Wrath's phone. A sound like the buzzing of an air conditioner or maybe the hum of electronics filled the air. It lent an eerie quality to our already creepy surroundings. Gradually, my eyes adjusted to the darkness, and when I realized what I was seeing, my heart fell into my stomach.

"What the hell is this place?" Envy asked aloud.

"It looks like some kind of laboratory," Sloth answered.

Wrath found a light switch and flipped it. Fluorescent lights buzzed on, casting the room in a cool, white light. The room was large and square, maybe 60 x 60 feet. In the middle stood long metal tables laden with scientific equipment: Beakers, Bunsen burners, microscopes, flasks, and test tubes. The floor was clean linoleum tile. There was no dust anywhere—it seemed the place had been recently used. It appeared, like Sloth said, to be a chemist's laboratory.

That is, until I saw the cages.

Locked, metal enclosures of varying sizes were stacked against the walls. Some were small, maybe rabbit-sized, while others were large enough to contain a pair of full-grow people. These larger cages were additionally outfitted with chains and handcuffs that hung from the tops of the cell. Dark stains marred the floor around some of the larger corrals. I looked away, swallowing around the huge lump in my throat. If that was blood, I didn't want to know about it.

On the far side of the room, another empty cage sat apart from the rest. It was large, big enough for a person. It was outfitted with a neatly made cot, a water pitcher, and, strangely, an icebox containing fresh, raw ocean fish. Unlike the other cages, this one looked like it hadn't been used.

"Tell me this isn't what I think it is," Wrath said.

"This is Chenoweth property," I said. "This is where they bring the supernaturals."

As soon as I spoke the words aloud, I knew them to

be true. I thought back to when I'd found Ping in the alleyway, her eyes wild with fear. "You don't know what they do to my kind," she said, terrified. "Experiments. Torture."

Experiments. Torture.

Her words rang through me as I took in the totality of my surroundings. This was the place Ping was so afraid of. This was the place we'd been looking for. The star on the map didn't note Déjà Brew at all.

It marked this place. *This* was the Nexus of Power.

I was about to suggest that we split up to search the hidden laboratory when a scream ripped through the room. My head shot up, eyes flying wide as I whipped my head around, trying to locate the source of the sound.

"Over here!" Sloth ran to a corner of the room where something was covered with a quilted moving pad. She grabbed a corner and tugged until the blanket slipped to the ground, revealing a plain, metal birdcage. She gasped, hands flying to her mouth as she stared.

Inside the cage were two brightly colored sun conures.

"Pride! It's Mrs. Romanowsky's parrots," she exclaimed. "This proves it. This is Chenoweth. We've found their hideout. These are the birds they stole."

The birds were flapping wildly in their cage, screaming and banging their wings against their metal confines. Feathers flew everywhere. The enclosure was much smaller than the one Eleanor kept for them—this one was not much larger than a cat carrier.

Sloth grabbed the cage and hugged it to her chest,

her jaw set. "Tear this place apart if you have to. If there are any other supernaturals in here, we have to rescue them. Don't just stand there, guys. Get moving."

Sloth didn't need to ask twice. The four of us split up as we began our frantic search for more kidnapped supernaturals. We searched under tables, overturned boxes, threw open cabinets and closet doors, searching every nook and cranny. We couldn't leave a single creature behind. But after several minutes of frenzied hunting, we found nothing besides the parrots.

"What should we do now?" I asked once the laboratory was secured.

"We have to tell someone about this place," Sloth said. "Where exactly are we? What business connects to this place? We have to know—"

But Sloth's speech was interrupted when Wrath threw his hood away from his face, sniffing the air. "Do you guys smell that? It smells like—"

I sniffed the air. Hot metal. Melted plastic. Smoke.

The laboratory was filling with curls of black smoke. I spun around to see Envy at the back of the room with her hand buried in the roots of her hair, jaw clenched, her whole body shaking. And then I saw what loomed behind her—a towering pillar of fire with long, thin, humanoid limbs and a furious expression on its uncannily human face.

"Envy," I breathed, stark terror rising in my chest. "Tell me you didn't summon that. Tell me that's not one of your fire elementals."

"This place is evil," she said, her voice thick with rage. As she spoke, her skin lit up with the bright yellows and oranges of the flames burning behind her. "I don't have to let this stand. This place shouldn't be here. So I'm destroying it. This ends now."

No sooner were the words out of her mouth than the fire elemental exploded, raining a torrent of flame and burning ash down on the room, lighting the equipment, the walls, the furniture on fire.

"Envy!" I screamed. "What did you do? *What did you do?*"

The birds, too, were screaming, their fevered screeches matching my own. Sloth clutched the cage tighter to her chest and turned her back, protecting the birds from the inferno with her body. Wrath grabbed me by the wrist, hauling me across the room as we dodged the flames burning hot and furious around us. "No time for lectures, man," he cried. "We gotta get outta here! Like, *pronto!*"

We ran. The laboratory had to be connected to a street-level room the same way the Crypt was connected to Déjà Brew. But though we searched every corner, we couldn't find any door leading up and out of the underground. The heat in the laboratory was terrifying. The fire was spreading so much faster than I would have thought possible. I pressed my nose into the crook of my arm, eyes watering as I searched for an escape.

"We have to go back into the tunnels." Sloth was shouting over the roar of the fire growing around us. "There's no other way out."

"If we go back into the tunnels, we'll die for sure," Wrath shot back. "All the doors we found were locked!"

"We didn't search everywhere," I said, trying to keep

my cool. That was becoming more and more difficult as the conflagration closed in. "There might be another exit. Sloth's right; we can't stay here. Let's go!"

We practically tripped over each other as we pushed our way out of the laboratory and back into the tunnels. Wrath had the good sense to close the door behind us. Maybe that would contain the blaze for a little while. Maybe not. We ran down the twisting corridors in stark darkness, made all the more blind by our fire-seared retinas. I fumbled my phone from my pocket, trying to thumb on the flashlight. But I was shaking so badly, the device slipped from my fingers and crashed to the ground. The glass interface shattered.

"Up here!" Wrath shouted ahead. I snatched up my phone, sticking it in my pocket as I dashed to catch up with my housemate.

"What did you find?" Sloth was breathless, her fingers gone bloodless as she squeezed the wire of the cage in her grasp.

Wrath was standing before a metal grating about half the height of a normal door. He kneeled down and pried his fingers into the gaps and tugged. The grating came loose, revealing a narrow crawlspace just large enough to traverse if we hunched down. We scrambled into the cramped space with Wrath leading the way and Sloth and the parrots bringing up the rear. At last, the corridor emptied out into another hallway, at the end of which stood a stairwell leading up. We rushed up the stairs to find a rusted metal door locked from the other side. Wrath shouted at the lock and pulled the handle.

The door groaned open.

Quaking with adrenaline and relief, we poured through, panting and sweating, to find ourselves on the street on the other side of the building from where we'd started.

"Is everybody okay?"

Sloth's teeth were chattering. She was still clutching the bird cage tight against her chest. Her face was smudged, maybe with dirt, maybe soot. I couldn't tell in the pale starlight. The night air smelled of smoke and chemicals. I guess closing the door didn't do as much good as I hoped.

"We're fine," Envy answered for the group, looking us all over. She scrubbed her face with her palms. "We're all okay."

"No thanks to you," I spat. "How do you keep *doing* that? We could have died back there! Why can't you—"

"Maybe later for this," Sloth interrupted. "We have to get back to the house. We're all on the edge of shock, and it's gonna hit real soon. No one should be behind the wheel when that happens."

No one argued further. We headed swiftly for the car, heads bent low against the night. I reached into my pocket for my phone, yanking it free. As I peered down into the shattered screen, I saw how badly I was shaking. Sloth was right. We were all in for a bad night.

But it could be worse. After all, we were lucky. We were alive.

Thank you for the good luck, Gluttony, I thought as I climbed into the car and slammed the door, listening to the distant wail of sirens growing nearer.

———

The next morning came way too quickly. I'd watched each hour tick by on the alarm clock on my nightstand as I trembled beneath my sheets. I'd still been awake at 6 a.m., but I didn't remember seeing 7, so maybe that was around the time I finally fell asleep.

Either way, it was still too early when a knock came at my door.

Wonderful, I thought. *My housemates finally learned to knock and it's at the most inopportune time.* I pulled myself to seated and rubbed the sleep from my eyes.

"Come in," I croaked.

The door opened slowly, and when I saw who stood at the entrance, I knew I was about to have a very bad day.

Detective Doyle stepped into my room and closed the door behind him. He looked me up and down. "Rough night?" he asked.

I faked nonchalance with a shallow lift of my shoulders. "Oh, you know how it goes. We Hollywood types are always looking to have a good time. I guess we had too much fun last night."

The lie came effortlessly, but I felt like a schmuck saying it aloud, especially because I could see all over the detective's face that he didn't believe a word. However, he didn't call my bluff. He remained standing in the corner, arms folded over his chest. "I'm here about your tip," he said.

Tip? What tip? I was so groggy and hungover from

the previous night's adrenaline that I could barely think straight. "What are you talking about?"

"Portia's alibi is airtight," he said. "The night Ed Thornton was shot, Portia was having dinner with the mayor. At least half a dozen people saw her."

I rubbed my face with my palms, trying to wake up. I didn't dare stand— I couldn't even remember what I was wearing. If I somehow had on my favorite unicorn pajamas, I would die of mortification. "Okay," I said. "So it wasn't Portia. Good, I guess. You came all the way here to tell me that?"

Now, the detective stepped closer to me, his expression darkening. "Not exactly," he said. "Let's be frank with each other, Pride. One investigator to another. I might not be a psychic, but I've been doing this job for a long time. And when you've been on the streets for as long as I have, you develop intuition about people. There's something you're not telling me, and I want to know what it is."

I shook my head, refusing to meet the detective's eyes. "I have no idea what you're talking about. Everything I know about this case, I've told you." That was a lie. I was sure Edgar's murder and Eleanor's murder were linked, and I hadn't shared anything with the detective about that. But it was too early and I was too messed up to get into it now. "That was the deal, right?"

Detective Doyle nodded. "It was the deal, all right. I'm just not sure you're holding up your end of it."

I sighed. "Look, detective. Can we do this later? I could use a shower and some coffee. And some, you know. Clothes."

"Would you prefer to do this at the station?" A snide smile quirked over his lips.

"That wouldn't be my first choice," I admitted, "but right now, I'd rather be anywhere than half naked in my bed being interrogated by the cops." Especially the night after my comrades and I had accidentally-on-purpose set downtown on fire.

The detective heaved a sigh and stuffed his hands into his pockets, rocking back onto his heels. "All right. If that's how you want to play this, I get it. You're holding your cards close to your chest. I have no evidence to suggest that you're withholding information about Ed's murder, but if that should change, please know I will not hesitate to arrest you. Big Hollywood star or no, I take my job seriously."

I felt even more like a schmo now that he used my own Hollywood line against me.

The detective turned to go. But just as he reached my door, he snapped his fingers and turned around. "I almost forgot." He walked over to the bed and withdrew something from his hip pocket, tossing it into my lap.

It was a wallet. *My* wallet.

I stared at it, frosty dread climbing from my stomach into my throat. When I looked up again to meet the detective's eyes, he wasn't smiling.

"Found that on the street in Old Downtown," he said. "I guess you heard about the fire."

I closed my eyes and let my chin fall to my chest. My heart was pounding so loud, I was sure the detective could hear. The stupid wallet must have fallen from my pocket when I'd been fumbling around with my phone.

"I don't know what you're talking about," I managed. "What fire?"

"Old Downtown burned last night," he said. "Whole town's talking about it. Weird that you didn't hear."

I scoffed. "I just woke up, detective."

The detective grunted noncommittally. "I see. So then, I guess this is the part where you tell me you don't know where or when you dropped that."

I didn't trust myself to speak. I could've dropped that wallet at any time—it didn't mean anything. The detective had to know that.

And I had a feeling he *did* know that—and more he wasn't sharing.

I gave a slow shake of my head. "No idea," I squeaked out.

The detective clucked his tongue against his cheek and turned to go. "That's too bad, Pride," he said. "If you think of anything, you have my number."

And in the next moment, he was gone.

twelve

. . .

"**E**nvy, what the star-spangled devil were you thinking?"

Of course, I didn't say 'star-spangled devil.' I said something more explicit that isn't polite to repeat in mixed company. The four of us were huddled together in Sloth's room, me pacing back and forth while Envy perched on the foot of Sloth's bed, arms crossed over her chest, a deep frown scribbled over her features. Sloth was at her desk, her bathrobe half-tied at her waist, cheek propped against her fist. Wrath was standing in the corner, his hoodie pulled low over his face and his hands dug into his pockets. All of us were on edge. Well, maybe not Sloth. I wasn't sure she had any edges.

"I don't see what the big deal is," Envy said for the third time that morning. "You saw that place. Those people were doing unthinkable things down there. To animals or people or shapeshifters—it doesn't matter. I saw cages, handcuffs, and blood with my own eyes, Pride. And so did you. I did what had to be done."

"You burned down an entire historical district!" I shouted, throwing my hands in the air. "Don't you have the slightest remorse about that?"

Envy shot me a dark look. "No! And keep your voice down! We don't need the whole house knowing what we did."

"What *you* did!" I fired back.

"You know what I *do* feel bad about?" she continued. "Evil organizations getting away with murder because people like you and me are too chicken to do anything about them. So last night, I did something about it."

Incredulity made my voice shake. "But you burned up all of our evidence, too! If we had gone to the police, they could have done a proper investigation. We could've looked for fingerprints. Some telltale sign of the people behind the evil we found down in the tunnels. But your fire obliterated all of that. My goodness, Envy, depending on how you look at it, you actually did the criminals a favor!"

Sloth yawned and fluttered her eyes sleepily. "Guys?"

"I hate to say it," Wrath said, "but I agree with Envy, man. We didn't find anything illegal down there. It's not like we found a meth lab. We found some birds. If we'd turned the case over to the authorities, what could they have done? They'd probably need a search warrant or whatever, man. And by the time all that went down, the bad guys woulda cleared outta there anyway. And let's say the cops did go down there," Wrath pressed on. "What would they have done? Probably just fined those guys or something. And that's the problem, man. Fines disproportionately hurt the poor more than the rich. Until we start enacting fines as a percentage of income, then—"

I dug my hands into my hair, my frustration mounting. "But we're not talking about poor versus rich, Wrath! Listen to yourself! How do you manage to turn every conversation into some anti-capitalism rant? Envy burned down the Chenoweth laboratory and any potential evidence along with it! How are we supposed to catch the guys behind this now?"

"You're blowing this out of proportion," Envy said. "I destroyed their secret base. So we didn't catch them this time. But we hit them where it hurts, and that counts for something."

"I don't want to hear another word from you," I snapped, pointing a finger in Envy's face. "You've got an answer for everything. How about accepting some personal responsibility, huh?"

My housemate gaped. "Are you seriously lecturing me about personal responsibility? You're the one who can't apologize even when you're *clearly* in the wrong! If you had just apologized to your stupid girlfriend, you wouldn't even be in this mess in the first place!"

My face flushed hot with fury and embarrassment. "So you admit it's a mess!" I thundered. "Now admit it's *your* mess, Envy! You and your stupid elemental—"

Sloth cleared her throat. "Guys?"

"I don't have to sit here and listen to this," Envy said, climbing to her feet. "I did what I did and I'm not sorry. If you've got a problem with me, Pride, take it up with the network. Maybe Tricia will give you a new partner."

"Oh, I'm already thinking about it," I fumed. "I'd rather forfeit this round than spend another minute—"

"*Guys!*"

We were so unused to the sound of Sloth raising her voice that the room fell silent as all heads turned toward her. Her cheek was still propped against her fist, but her face was red now, her mouth pulled into a frown. "Can we talk about this later? We have more pressing issues to deal with."

We all followed Sloth's gaze to the cage sitting in the corner of her room. She'd covered the birdcage with a blanket, and the parrots were blessedly quiet—so quiet, we'd forgotten about them. "So. What are we going to do about the birds?" she asked.

"Well, I guess we should get them out of that Magic-Bloc cage," Wrath said. "Then…well, I guess we'll see. I'll go see if we have any wire cutters."

While Wrath disappeared from the room, Envy sat back down on the bed, and I took in a deep breath to calm my nerves. "I didn't mean to shout at you," I said. It was the closest thing to an apology she was going to get, and I hoped she appreciated that. "It's just you put us in a really bad position. You know the detective was here this morning?"

Now Envy's eyes widened in surprise. "Detective Doyle? He was here? Why?"

I scoffed. "Ostensibly, to tell me Portia's alibi checked out. She wasn't the one who shot Edgar. But he also wanted to drop this off." I tossed my wallet onto the bed. When Envy saw it, her hand drew to her mouth, and the color seeped from her face.

"Oh no," she breathed. "That's not your wallet, is it?"

"He knows we were there," I answered. "Or at least, he knows I was. And if he's on to me, there's a good chance he's onto the rest of us."

"You could've lost that wallet last week for all he knows," Envy said. "That's not enough evidence to put us in trouble, is it?"

I shrugged. "I don't know. On its own, probably not. But I'm guessing the detective knows more than he's letting on. So what I'm saying is, this wouldn't have happened if you hadn't loosed that ridiculous elemental on the town."

Envy opened her mouth to object, but Sloth held up her hand and snapped her fingers. "Not again," she said. "If you guys want to argue about this, take it to another room. What's done is done. We're a team. If one of us goes down, we all go down. So we need to have each other's backs."

The bedroom door opened, and Wrath slipped inside, a pair of wire cutters in his hand. He strode over to the birdcage and lifted the blanket, tossing it to the ground. The parrots chirped enthusiastically as Wrath took to the cage, grunting and swearing as he worked at the wires. A moment later, I heard it: the snap of metal as Wrath pulled the side panel free and dropped it to the floor.

The birds huddled in the corner of the cage, not

moving. "Come on now, you stupid birds," Wrath said. "Cage is open. Just come out, will you?"

Sloth giggled from her chair. "Just take them out, Wrath. You're not afraid of them, are you? They're just parrots. They can't hurt you."

Pushing up the sleeves on his hoodie, Wrath reached into the cage. The birds danced away from him, but they couldn't move far. The cage was only so big. Finally, Wrath lifted one in his hand and withdrew it, placing it on the carpet. He reached in for the second bird and placed it beside the first. The parrots were stunned motionless and silent. But then one parrot lifted its foot, and I noticed the silver rings on their feet.

"Sloth, do you have anything we can cut these little coils with? The wire cutters are too big."

Sloth went to her bedside table and retrieved a pair of nail clippers. "Will these work?"

I took the clippers and carefully pinched at the metal until the birds' feet were free. At first, nothing happened. But slowly, the parrots began to shimmer as a faint light bloomed around them. There was a sound like a light-bulb popping, and the birds snapped together like magnets, melding to each other at the sides. Gradually, the parrots began to transform, blending into each other as the prismatic light pulsed and grew brighter until I had to turn away to save my eyes. When I looked back, I shrieked.

Sitting on the floor stark naked was…

… *Portia Cameron?!*

I stared at Portia with my mouth agape, unable to process what I was seeing. When she realized she was naked, Portia drew her arms over her chest and turned away from us, a pink blush crawling up her neck and into her cheeks. Sloth jumped to her feet, retrieved the blanket that had been on the parrot cage, and draped it over the woman's shoulders. Portia gathered the blanket around her and looked up into Sloth's face, gratitude blooming all over her features. Her eyes were wide and glassy, and she looked enchanted. Or hungover. Or something.

But this didn't make sense. How could the parrots be Portia? I'd just seen her!

Tentatively, I stepped toward her. "Portia?"

Portia looked up at me and blinked. She opened her mouth as though trying to speak, but no words came out. She bit down on her lip and drew a deep breath, trying again. "What day is it?" she managed finally.

"Tuesday, I think," I said.

Portia's brow furrowed, and a shadow passed over her features. Then she said, "Sorry. The date? Can you please tell me the date?"

My housemates and I exchanged nervous glances. Envy walked over to the woman and kneeled beside her, placing a hand on her forehead. She whispered something in Portia's ear, and the woman froze. "That can't be right," she breathed, shaking her head in denial. "That would mean…that would mean I was in that cage for over a year."

I stared at her, my mind reeling. Finally, I blurted, "Portia, what are you talking about? What's going on?"

The woman tightened the blanket around her shoulders. "I'm not Portia," she said. "I'm Peyton. Portia and I are twins."

I stared mutely until the words made sense. Peyton. I recognized that name—I'd heard Portia say it in Detective Doyle's office. They'd been arguing about the existence of the supernatural, and the detective had maintained it was nothing but fancy. And Portia had shot back, "Then explain Peyton."

I gave a long blink. This was Peyton. Portia's twin sister.

Portia's twin sister was a supernatural.

I was only beginning to register the implications of this revelation when Envy walked across the room to Sloth's closet and pulled out a stained but otherwise clean sweatshirt and a pair of dark leggings. She handed these to Peyton. "Why don't you get dressed," she said, keeping her voice soft. "We need to get you somewhere safe."

Peyton accepted the clothing with a bashful twist of her lips. "Can you take me to my sister? Please?"

I pulled out my phone. "I'm on it. What's her number?"

Peyton gave me her sister's number, and I dialed as we filed out of the room to give her some privacy. In the hallway, I leaned against a wall, phone pressed to my ear.

"Portia Cameron's phone," an assistant answered.

"Put Portia on," I said. "It's an emergency."

"I'm sorry, but Portia—"

"Put her on immediately or so help me I will hunt your whole family down."

That did the trick. A moment later, a disgruntled Portia was on the other end, breathing loudly into the phone. "Who is this? I'm in the middle of—"

"Portia, this is Pride. Please don't interrupt. Meet me at your house in fifteen minutes." I sighed, closing my eyes. "I can't explain over the phone. You wouldn't believe me if I did. Just be there. I have something you want. Don't be late." I disconnected without waiting for a reply. To my housemates, I said, "This day's gonna need coffee. Lots of it."

I was heading toward the kitchen when Envy sidled up to me and tugged on my sleeve. "Can we talk?" When I didn't stop walking, she caught up with me, matching my pace. "I know you're angry with me right now," she began, "but let me come with you to Portia's. I know this isn't part of our case, but I'd really like to see the two sisters reunited."

I narrowed my eyes at her. "This isn't one of your 'get-famous-on-TikTok' schemes, is it? I'm not letting you use their tragedy for personal gain, Envy."

My housemate's face darkened, her mouth drawing into a hard line. "Whatever else you may think about me, Pride, I would hope you know I have common decency. Yeah, I want to be social media famous, but I'm not a monster."

I hesitated, examining her face. I don't know what I was looking for—under the best circumstances, I couldn't tell what people were thinking or feeling. But Envy looked sincere. And while I *was* angry with her, I knew she wasn't a monster.

"All right," I said, softening only a little. "You can come. I'll see if Sloth wants to come, too."

While Envy disappeared into her room to get dressed, I found Sloth downstairs. She was in the kitchen making breakfast—coffee with jam on toast. She left a trail of crumbs everywhere, and she'd dribbled heavy creamer all over the counter. She didn't even seem to notice. But after the night and morning we'd just had, I figured extending a little grace was the least I could do.

"Envy and I are taking Peyton over to Portia's," I said. "Do you want to come? After all, this is all part of the Romanowsky case. And that case was yours from the beginning."

But Sloth moaned, shaking her head. "No, thank you. I've had more than enough excitement for a while. You guys go. I'm feeling overwhelmed, and I need to recharge my social batteries." She offered me a smile, but I noticed for the first time the half-moons beneath her eyes. She really did look wrung out.

"All right," I said. I reached for the coffee, pouring myself a mug. "So, can I ask you something?"

"Sure," she said. "What's up?"

"I was wondering." I took a sip of the coffee. It was too hot to drink, but I was stalling. "The other day at City Hall, you mentioned you saw Pam's thoughts because they were, you know. Right there." I cleared my throat. "Have you ever…I don't know, accidentally picked up on Lust's thoughts? You know, because they're *right there?*"

Sloth took a bite of toast, leaving a smear of jam on

the tip of her nose. "I pick up stuff from everyone," she said. "You guys are all very loud thinkers."

That got me blushing, but I tried not to focus on it. If I went down the rabbit hole of which of my thoughts Sloth had picked up, I'd surely wind up buried alive. "Well, I was wondering if you ever heard Lust thinking about me. And if she does think about me, well…"

"You want to know how she feels about you," Sloth finished.

"Yes," I breathed, relieved I didn't have to spell it out. I felt like I was in 6th grade again, sliding notes to my crush's best friend. "Does Lust like me? Check Yes or No."

Honestly, having feelings is so undignified.

Sloth sighed and licked her lips. "I can't tell you that, Pride. It wouldn't be ethical. But here's the thing. You don't need a mind-reader to find out if Lust likes you. All you have to do is *talk* to her."

"I can't," I said, shrugging lamely as I stepped away. "I wouldn't be able to get the words out. Emotions, relationships…they're not really my strong suit," I said.

"Avoiding rejection is a lonely way to live," Sloth said from around another mouthful of jam and toast. "Sometimes, you have to be vulnerable. You know, I can help you with that."

I quirked an eyebrow. "Really? How?"

Sloth grinned. "In my day job, I'm a professional cuddler. I hold people and make them feel safe and secure. I could do that for you if you want."

My mouth dropped open. "You're a…*what?* You hug people for a living?"

Sloth nodded. "It's low energy, and I'm good at it. Do you want—"

"No," I said, a little louder than I meant to. "Thanks, but that sounds like a nightmare. No offense."

Sloth shrugged lightheartedly. "None taken. Well, if you change your mind, you know where to find me. It's not as weird as you might think. It can be very therapeutic."

I heard a sound and turned to find Peyton coming into the kitchen. She was dressed in Sloth's oversized sweatshirt that hung limply from one shoulder and baggy leggings that bunched around her ankles. It was only after seeing her fully clothed that I realized how thin she was. As parrots, she'd looked healthy. As a human, she was little more than skin and bones. A sharp collarbone peeked out from her shirt. Her cheeks were gaunt, her undereyes gray and sunken. Maybe she'd always been thin, but there was *thin,* and there was *emaciated*.

When she saw me looking, Peyton blushed, glancing down at her outfit. "I've never stayed in animal form for so long," she said, trying to smile. She looked like a scared child. "I guess it took a toll on my body. But I'm sure I'll fill out again eventually."

I said nothing and looked away. Whoever had done this to her would pay.

"Thank you for the clothes," she said to Sloth. "I promise to return them."

Sloth shook her head and sipped her coffee. "Keep them. I'm just glad you're safe."

"Okay," Envy said, jogging into the kitchen. "I'm

ready." For a delinquent who had just summoned an elemental to torch all of Old Downtown, she looked remarkably like a retiree on a cruise. She wore a pair of linen culottes and a blue and white striped boatneck shirt. Her freshly Botoxed face completed the look. "Let's get this show on the road."

When we pulled into Portia's driveway ten minutes later, Peyton pressed her hands to her mouth, her eyes wide. "It looks just how I remember," she breathed. "She's redone her landscaping, it looks like. But otherwise, it's the same. How can so little have changed?"

I didn't have an answer for that, so I said nothing. We got out of the car and marched up to the house. As we approached, Peyton lagged behind, cowering after me. I paused to look at her, noticing the way her lips trembled and her eyes darted around. "Are you all right? Is this what you want to do?"

Peyton hesitated a moment before biting down on her lip and giving a crisp nod. "Yes. I'm just scared, is all."

I offered what I hoped was a reassuring smile. "There's nothing to be afraid of," I said. "Come on. Let's get you home."

I pressed the doorbell.

A few moments later, the front door flew open. Portia's expression was stony, her cheeks flaming red. By the way she bared her teeth, I could tell she was ready to issue me an epic tongue lashing. *Nobody tells Portia Cameron what to do!* and *Who do you think you are?* and all that jazz. But the moment she saw her sister, Portia froze in the doorway. All her ferocity melted away, and she stared in blank shock. A protracted silence followed, and then finally, Portia whispered, "Peyton?"

No one said another word. Portia rushed forward, pulling her sister into a fierce embrace. Peyton pressed her face into the crook of her twin sister's neck, and the two women huddled together in the doorway and sobbed.

thirteen

. . .

Once the shock of seeing her sister wore off, Portia ushered us inside and took us into the living room. She instructed the house staff to prepare food while she situated her sister on the couch. She surrounded Peyton with comfortable pillows and fluffy blankets, even though it wasn't cool in the house. Peyton welcomed them, however, burrowing down in them like a small animal.

Portia nestled into the couch beside her sister, taking her twin's hands in her own. The stark difference in their weight was made evident when Portia's fingers, nearly chubby by comparison, caressed her sister's skeletal phalanges. "I never thought I would see you again," Portia said. Her voice was raw with emotion. "You were gone for a whole year, Peyton. *An entire year.*"

Peyton nodded and sniffled, wiping away a stray tear that had leaked onto her cheek. "I know. They told me. I can't believe it's been that long. But you know, time passes differently for me when I'm…" She glanced over at Envy and me as stricken panic flashed over her face.

"We know about shapeshifters," I said softly. "It's a long story, but we know. And don't worry. Your secret is safe with us."

At my words, Peyton relaxed slightly and nodded, returning her attention to Portia. "Anyway, I don't remember much. I suppose that's probably a blessing, given the way I look." She glanced down at her body, and I assumed she was referring to her weight. "Nothing hurts, though. I don't see any scars or anything. So they couldn't have hurt me too badly."

"They stole a year of your life," Portia cut in, her words punctuated by palpable anger. "They took you away from your family. That's time we can never get back. So maybe they didn't leave any visible marks, Peyton, but they hurt you terribly. You and me both."

Peyton shuddered and pulled the blanket tighter around her body. "I guess you're right," she said.

Softening her voice, Portia asked, "Do you remember anything? Do you remember who took you— who is responsible?"

Peyton squeezed her eyes shut, doing her best to conjure up a helpful memory. "I remember a little. Charmaine Young and I had gone shopping at the city-wide garage sale. She wanted to find some vintage curtains, and I'd never been to city-wide before. It sounded like fun. We took Charmaine's car. I guess we'd been shopping for a little over an hour when I got hungry. I went over to concessions while Charmaine kept shopping. After I ate, I had to pee, so I went to the ladies' room. And before I even made it to a stall, a man grabbed me from behind. He slapped handcuffs on my wrists and I…" She sniffled and pressed her knuckles into her eye. "I shifted."

"Do you know who it was, Peyton?" Portia was rubbing her sister's back, her voice as soft as feathers. "Was it someone you knew?"

"It was Walt Romanowsky," I said. "When she was parrots, I saw her at his house. I didn't know it was her, of course. I didn't know they were supernatural parrots for that matter." I turned to Peyton. "But then someone kidnapped you from Walt's house, right? And they took you underground. Do you know who?"

Peyton shook her head. "No. They wore masks. But I'm pretty sure one of them was a woman. Two men and a woman," she repeated, as though confirming this with herself.

I nodded, deep in thought as I considered everything Peyton shared. "So, Charmaine was the last person to see you before you disappeared," I mused aloud. "Portia, did the police ever interview her? Did Doyle?"

"This is the first I'm hearing that my sister was even with Charmaine," Portia admitted.

Now, Peyton frowned, her chin wobbling as she looked up into her sister's face. "No, that can't be right. She must have reported me missing. When she couldn't find me that day? We went to the event together," she insisted. "She must have looked for me. And then when she didn't find me, surely she came to you. Right? I mean, you'd be the first person she'd call."

Raw anger crept up Portia's spine, changing her

body language and blooming crimson in her face. "She never called me," Portia whispered through a clenched jaw. "I had no idea she was with you. I had no idea you'd been taken from city-wide garage sale. All I knew was you were gone. I didn't know *what* happened to you. I suspected your disappearance had to do with your ability. Mom and Dad always said if anyone found out about you, it could be dangerous. But it was only unfounded suspicion."

"Portia," I drawled, "is that why you wanted me to be on the lookout for supernatural involvement on the Edgar Thornton case?" I asked. "Did you think maybe I'd find something that would lead to your sister?"

Portia sniffled, new tears seeping from her eyes. "I never thought I'd see Peyton again," she admitted. "But yes. Tell me you don't see a connection. Wights? Talking corpses? A traveling statue? A sister who can shift into an animal? Don't you think all of this is somehow related?"

"Yes." I answered before I even realized I would, and I didn't know until I said it that I believed it. "I don't know how. But yes. It's Odyssey."

"I hate it," Portia spat. "I hate it all. I lost a year of my sister's life because of…what? The paranormal? The supernatural? I want it all gone. Whatever it takes to root it out of my home, I'll do it. I will burn Odyssey's supernatural proclivities to the ground."

"Don't say that," Peyton said, snuggling into her sister's arms. "This is our home. And it's weird but it's wonderful. So don't say that. Don't even think it. We don't know why I am the way I am, but I'm still me."

"Well, I know one thing," Portia said, hugging her twin tight. "We know Charmaine knew something. I never considered her a friend, but I never would have thought she'd be complicit in your disappearance."

"She wasn't complicit," Peyton objected. "At least, I have no reason to believe—"

"She didn't *say* anything, Peyton! She should have gone directly to the police! To Kelly! To me! But she never said a *word.*"

"We should go talk to her," I said to Envy.

But as I got to my feet, Portia peeled away from her sister and stood, shaking her head sternly. "No. I know I told Kelly to let you help, but you've done enough. This is kidnapping and conspiracy and heaven knows what else. Now isn't the time for an amateur investigation. It was reckless of me to let you get involved in the first place."

"You might be right about that," I agreed. "But please, Portia. Charmaine's also a suspect in Edgar Thornton's murder. With everything else that's been happening, we haven't had a chance to dig into it. But we want answers, too."

Portia's face darkened. "If she's involved in a kidnapping *and* a murder, that's more reason to stay far away from her. Let the professionals handle it."

"Pride *is* a professional," Envy said. "If you want to get to the bottom of this—and I know you do—there's no one better to have on your team than Pride. I ought to know."

For a moment, I was speechless. Even after the way I'd treated her that morning, Envy still had my back. I was so moved by her small praise that I just stood there gaping. But I finally came to my senses and touched Portia lightly on the arm. "Just give me a head start on the cops. Envy and I will head over to Charmaine's right now. Envy's good with people. It's a gift—she gets them to talk."

The steely determination in Portia's face remained a second longer but then melted away as her shoulders sagged and she nodded. "Fine. I guess I owe you that much. But I'm only giving you a few minutes head start before I call Kelly. So whatever you want to ask her, you better ask her soon as you see her. Because I intend to put that cow away for the rest of her life for what she did to my family. Do you understand?"

Envy and I were already heading for the front door. "Understood. Ten minutes, Portia. Ten minutes."

And with that, Envy and I bolted out the door.

Charmaine lived in a quaint area of Odyssey, one of the older parts of town that hadn't been revamped to be some sort of Hollywood beach town fantasy. It looked like a place where normal people lived. Well, normal people and a possible shapeshifting seal, but still.

"What's the address again?" I asked.

Envy looked down into her phone. "1821 Seabreeze Way."

I pointed to a pink-and-white stucco house with a patchy grass yard and a classic Cadillac parked in the driveway. "It's this one," I said. "I would have thought

Charmaine would live in something…I don't know, grander."

Envy unbuckled her seatbelt and opened the door. "Let's not sit here lollygagging. We only have a 10-minute head start, remember? The cops will be here any minute. Hop to it."

We strode up to Charmaine's door. I had no idea what I wanted to say—I just knew I had to get the truth out of Charmaine before the cops arrived. If she knew anything about Chenoweth, I had to get that information from her. Who knew how many others might be in danger? I thought of the bounty page on the Chenoweth website and shuddered. There were so many creatures listed.

No, not creatures. People.

I pounded on the door. "Charmaine! It's me, Pride! We have to talk."

There was no answer.

"We don't have time for this," Envy said. She tried the doorknob, and the door swung open. We barged into the house but didn't get very far before we both drew up short. My heart sank through the floor.

The house had been ransacked. There was no furniture overturned like at Mrs. Romanowsky's, but knick-knacks and tchotchkes that had been placed on the mantel and wall shelves were knocked to the ground. A glass table in the middle of the living room lay shattered.

I didn't need to be a detective to know that a struggle had taken place here.

"Search the house," I instructed.

Without arguing, Envy began shouting for Charmaine, going in and out of rooms before finally running up the stairs. While Envy searched, I examined the carnage looking for clues. It didn't take long to find what I was looking for.

Standing conspicuously upright in a room filled with things lying broken on their sides was a used canister of MagicBloc fogger.

Envy came running down the steps. "She's not here," she said. "She's gone."

"Chenoweth was here," I said. "They kidnapped her."

"Kidnapped?" The word hung heavy in the air between us. "Why? Why would they kidnap Charmaine?"

I paused. "I heard a rumor she might be a shapeshifter. Looks like the others might have heard the same thing."

Dizzy with this revelation, Envy was about to sink down onto the couch, but I caught her and shook her. "This is a crime scene," I said. "You can't sit on or touch anything. In fact, we should get out of here." I didn't wait for an argument as I hauled her out the front door.

Outside, I heard car doors slamming and I cursed, glancing down at my watch. That was the fastest ten minutes on earth. Detective Doyle met us on the sidewalk, his face a mask of fury. I jammed my thumb over my shoulder. "Something's happened to Charmaine," I said. "She's not there. It looks like someone took her."

"Someone?" The detective's eyes were wide and round, and a fire burned behind his irises. I half-expected smoke to shoot from his ears. "What are you *doing* here? How is it that everywhere I look, you turn up?"

I faltered. "Detective—"

"No, I don't have time for this. I'll deal with you later." The detective elbowed past me and strode into Charmaine's house.

Alone again, Envy turned to me, her hands twisting at her chest. "What do we do now?"

"We have to find the people behind Chenoweth," I said. Then I cursed and shot Envy a dirty look.

Envy's eyes narrowed. "Why are you looking at me like that?"

"I hate to remind you of this after so short a time, but we would know exactly where they would have taken her if you hadn't *burned it to the ground.*"

Without warning, Envy punched me in the shoulder before shoving me aside and stalking to the car. "I guess everything's my fault!" she shouted, her back to me. "Go ahead and blame me for it all!"

I sighed and dropped my chin to my chest. While Envy threw a tantrum, the detective came out of the house, his cell phone pressed against his ear. "I need a crime scene unit here immediately," he said. "Charmaine Young is missing. A cursory perusal of her home suggests possible abduction."

The detective disconnected and slipped his phone away, never tearing his eyes away from mine. "Let me be very clear," he said. "I don't want to see you at any more of my crime scenes. I don't want to find your name attached to any more of my victims. I want you out of my way or there's going to be trouble. Do you understand what I'm saying to you?"

I held up my hands in virtual surrender. "I had nothing to do with this," I said. "You talked to Portia. You know what's going on. I was merely following up on what Peyton said happened to her."

Anger flashed behind the detective's eyes, and he stepped forward, his large frame looming over mine, a finger pointed threateningly at my chest. "It wasn't your place to come investigate," he hissed. "You should have let Portia call me immediately. Is this a game to you? No, wait. Don't answer that." His face transformed into a snarl, nostrils flaring as he stepped even closer to me. I fumbled backward in response. "I know the real reason you're here. You're just a no-account D-lister hoping for your 15 minutes of fame and some *ridiculous* wish you think a TV network can grant you. But if you muck up one more of my cases, I'll make your life a living hell, and nothing anyone can offer you will be worth it. I promise you that."

I swallowed around the lump in my throat. I'd been talked down to by police officers before. It was never a walk in the park—I mean, they're cops. Half their job is to be intimidating. But this time was different because I felt something more than low-grade fear.

I felt *sad*.

For one thing, the detective had completely misjudged me. Yes, I was on this cockamamie TV show to win a prize. But that wasn't why I was *here*, standing in front of Charmaine's house. I was here because I cared. I was here because I wanted to see justice served. I wanted to be a force of good in a sea of human evil.

But it wasn't my job. Detective Doyle was not Detective Hidalgo, and Odyssey wasn't San Diego. Here, I was no one.

I mean, I was no one everywhere. I guess here, it was just more obvious.

"I understand, Detective Doyle. You won't see me again," I said. "I'll stay out of your way."

The detective gave a crisp nod. "Good. Now get out of here before I arrest you for—"

"Interfering with an ongoing investigation, yeah, I got it." I turned away from the detective, hands thrust into my pockets. I felt like a dog with its tail between its legs as I retreated to the car. When I got inside, I rested both hands on the steering wheel, leaning my head backward as I closed my eyes and let out a long, slow exhale.

"Everything okay?" Envy asked.

"I think we've worn out our welcome with the detective," I said. "Anything else we do regarding the Edgar Thornton case? We need to be stealthy about it. I don't want to give up," I said before Envy could object. "But we have to be careful. The detective threatened to arrest me if I get in his way one more time, and I believe him. So. The question is, what do we do now?"

"I think we should talk to the ghosts at Déjà Brew," Envy said. "Maybe one of them saw something. Someone going in or out of the secret passageway or something. It's worth a shot."

With my eyes still closed, I shook my head. "The

Crypt might not have burned down, but it's got to be badly damaged. Plus, the detective practically accused me of arson. We won't be allowed back over there."

I heard Envy shift in her seat as her seatbelt clicked. "Sounds like we'll just have to sneak in. Again."

I opened my eyes and looked over at her, expecting her to be smiling or giving some other indication that she was joking. But Envy looked dead serious. "Sneak into Déjà Brew *again?* Are you out of your mind? Didn't you just hear what I said about the detective?"

Envy shrugged. "I heard you. But do you have a better idea?"

"Yes. My better idea is to *not get arrested.*" I pinched the bridge of my nose. "Forget about Chenoweth for a minute," I said. "Let's focus on Edgar Thornton. What do you want to do about that?"

Envy smiled. "Same thing. When we were down in the Crypt, I found those meeting notes, remember? If there's a relationship between the Crypt and what was happening at Remembrance Home, the ghosts might know something about it."

I gripped the steering wheel until my knuckles turned white and hung my head to my chest. "You're just not gonna stop until I'm behind bars," I said, shaking my head in defeat. "And although I hate to say it, I think you may be right. No matter which case we investigate, all paths lead to Déjà Brew."

Envy turned her face away from mine and pressed her forehead to the window. "Well, good news is, the cops will be busy at Charmaine's for a while. So this is our chance. Breaking and entering, part two. This time with hopefully less fire damage."

I listened for a telltale sign that Envy was joking. But I got nothing.

"Too soon, Envy." I said. "Too soon."

Then I did the only thing I could do. I drove us back to Déjà Brew.

fourteen

. . .

Getting into Déjà Brew was easier the second time. We just walked in through the back door. Or rather, the lack of a back door. Inside, the walls were covered in soot, and I saw signs of water and smoke damage on the ceilings and floor. Counter tops were covered in soot and ash, and as we walked, we left a trail of footprints through the debris.

Great, I thought. *More evidence for the detective. Why don't I just leave my wallet here again?* But I kept my sarcasm to myself as Envy and I found our way down the steps and into the eerie darkness of the Crypt.

As expected, the room was badly damaged. The ceiling was crumbling, with tufts of pink insulation falling through. The walls were blackened, the paint bubbling on the surface. Much of the furniture had been surprisingly spared, but most of the books were destroyed, charred to nothingness.

Yet even among the wreckage, the ghosts still milled about almost as though nothing were wrong. As I surveyed the crowd looking for a familiar face, Eleanor floated over to me, her eyes liquid. Her fingers absently worried the string of pearls at her throat, and her lips trembled. "I'm so glad you're here," she said. She sounded breathless and rattled, like she'd been crying, though I wasn't sure ghosts could cry. "Damn not having a body! I'd like to give you a big hug. Well, no matter. I don't suppose you can spare an old woman some news? What happened here? How did the fire start? The reports I'm hearing are conflicting."

I took a sharp breath and avoided looking at Envy. It wasn't nearly as satisfying to poke her when she could only hear half the conversation. "Well, the details are a little murky. But I guess the fire started in another building and spread more quickly because of the underground tunnel system. Did you know about that? That Old Downtown is connected by a series of tunnels?"

Eleanor waved a hand. "Well, of course I knew that. All of us old-timers remember. We used to go on field trips through those tunnels when we were children."

"Is that right? Strange field trip, taking kids to see tunnels where criminals ferried illegal hooch."

Eleanor laughed and clucked her tongue playfully. "Now, see, that isn't what they told us children! They told us the tunnels were for electricity. Or maybe I remember that wrong. Well, my word. I guess you learn something new every day. And here I thought death itself imparted great wisdom! But I'm afraid I don't know much more today than when I kicked the bucket, pardon my language. Oh, ignore me, Pride," she said, her voice still full of apology. "I'm just a silly old woman."

"You're not old anymore," I reminded her. "You're dead. It's a very different thing."

Eleanor chuckled and waved a hand dismissively. "Oh, you."

"What's she saying?" Envy demanded.

"She doesn't know anything about the fire," I said. To Eleanor, I said, "Have you ever seen anyone using the tunnels? Going in or out of the secret passageway there?" I nodded toward the door we'd uncovered.

But Eleanor shook her head. "No, never."

I turned to Envy. "It's a negative on the secret passageway, too."

"Well, ask her what she knows about the talking corpses."

Eleanor's eyes widened. "Talking corpses?"

I explained briefly about the connection between the Society's meeting notes and the disturbances at Remembrance Home, but Eleanor just shook her head. "I'm sorry, I don't know anything about that. I haven't been down here that long, but maybe some of the others might know something."

"You're right," I said. "Thanks, Eleanor. Sloth sends her regards."

With Envy on my heels, I picked my way through the crowd, looking for someone who might want to talk, but most of the ghosts either ignored me or actively avoided me. Dead people were much like living people —they stuck to what they knew. And so I wasn't surprised when the only other ghost that seemed interested in my presence was Angelica.

When she saw me, she beckoned me over with a coy grin. "I thought I might see you here soon," she said. "Though I wasn't sure whether you'd be alive or dead when you returned."

I quirked my eyebrows. "Why?"

"Well, you went through that door and then the fire started. I never saw you come out. So I figured, you know." She sliced a finger across her throat and made a gross sound with her mouth.

"We found another way out," I explained. "Speaking of the passage, though, have you or any of the other ghosts ever seen anyone use that door in the Crypt? Ever seen anyone go in or come out?"

Angelica whistled. "No way. We were just as surprised as all of you when that bookcase slid away. Nobody's ever been in or out that door—not that any of us have noticed, anyway."

That wasn't the answer I hoped for, and my shoulders slumped in defeat. "Well, there goes that lead," I said.

"Things around here have been crazy," Angelica continued, unfazed by my downward turn. "Ghosts running around like chickens with their heads cut off. I mean, not literally. But you know what I mean."

"I'm surprised you're all still here," I said.

Angelica frowned. "Why?"

"Well, that's how you clear out unwanted ghosts and spirits and things. With smoke," I said.

"That's right," Envy chimed in. "Or air elementals."

I gave her a withering look. "Don't start."

"Well, I'm sure some of us would have moved on if we could have," Angelica said. "The thing about the Crypt though, is it seems to be where ghosts go when they don't have another choice. It's kind of like jail in that way. The accommodations are mediocre and the food isn't that great, but one is able to secure lodging instantly and without a reservation." She laughed and tossed her hair over a ghostly shoulder. "Seriously, though, where else are we supposed to go? Most of us are tethered here. There are only a few of us who have no trouble coming and going, and most of them have moved on. I took Fiona's departure especially hard. She was a gas."

I blinked. "Fiona Arquette? She was here?"

"Oh, sure. Crazy old bat. She used to amuse herself by scaring the pants off some of the others. She'd go invisible, sneak up on someone, and scream in their ear. You haven't lived until you've heard a ghost shout in fright." She chuckled at a memory. "Sometimes, she floated around here reciting Shakespeare in an English accent. You know, she was a ventriloquist, so I guess that's why she was so good with voices. Or maybe it's the other way around."

While Angelica had been talking, my brain was running a mile a minute, putting everything together. "Angelica, could Fiona leave the Déjà Brew?"

Again, Angelica nodded. "Yeah, she was one of the few that could. She liked to sneak out in the middle of the night like a teenager sneaking out to a party. At least, that's how I liked to think of it. It's fun to think that old Fiona was getting away with something."

A new realization struck me. "So…*she* was the one sneaking upstairs and shouting at the customers?"

Angelica laughed out loud, her shoulders shaking. "Oh man, that was *great!* You have to hand it to her— the old bat had a twisted sense of humor. By the time Felix started keeping the door to upstairs shut, it didn't matter anymore anyway. Fiona had already crossed over, and we never saw her again. God rest her soul."

"When?" I asked, my heart rate picking up. "When did Fiona cross over? Was it the same night Edgar Thornton was murdered?"

Angelica snapped her ghostly fingers and nodded. "You know what? Now that you mention it, yeah. I think it was."

I turned to Envy, a slow smile spreading on my face. "Envy, I think we finally got a break in this case. Let's go back to the house—I'll tell you everything, I promise. But first, I want to read those meeting minutes. That's the key to solving this whole mystery."

Envy squealed, bouncing on her toes and clapping her hands in glee. "So you know who killed Edgar?"

"No," I said, waving this away. "No idea. But I know why the corpses appeared to be talking."

Envy's excitement immediately drained away, and her shoulders sagged. "What? I thought we were supposed to be solving Edgar's murder?"

I reached out and pinched Envy on the cheek. "We just solved our assignment, Envy. You can thank me later, but you're one giant step closer to becoming America's Favorite Sin."

Envy squealed again and threw her arms around my neck. "I knew you were the best partner! I just knew it. Hang on." Envy pulled out her phone and drew herself close to me, her cheek pressed against mine. "Say cheese!"

She snapped a photo before I could object. She was typing furiously when she said, "I'm making the announcement on Instagram. There you go. It's official. We completed our assignment! And since I'm pretty sure we're the first, those Good Samaritan points are in the bag, baby!"

I was still standing there like a slack-jawed moron when Envy flew up the stairs. "You coming?" she called down.

I turned to Angelica. "Thanks for your help," I said. "If you want, I'll see what I can do about helping you cross over. I can't promise anything at all, but you've helped me, so I'd like to help you."

The ghost smiled and shook her head. "Thanks, but it's not a tit for tat thing, you know? You help people because it's the right thing to do. That's all." She blew me a kiss and a wink. "Just promise to keep visiting me. And whatever you do—keep kicking butt until *you* become America's Favorite Sin."

———

When we arrived back at Sinful House, I immediately retrieved the Society's meeting minutes and took the book back to my room. I hunkered down until I had read every page multiple times. With each read, a weight lifted from my shoulders. I liked when things made sense. And now, everything was adding up. Here's what I learned:

1. Whispers of real estate development meant the Society needed to find a new headquarters. This jibed with what I'd already heard from Felix.

2. The Society figured that if they could get a friend or colleague into office, they could move to the emergency shelter beneath City Hall which was private, secure, and unused.

3. Some Society members thought it would be better to make Old Downtown a historical landmark, which would protect Déjà Brew and the Crypt from development.

4. Someone objected (spoiler alert: it was Portia Cameron) that Old Downtown was prime real estate and had no historical value whatsoever.

5. Portia decided to formally run for mayor against Julian Gillespie. That caused a big fuss: half the Society members thought it was a great idea, while the other half worried Portia would sabotage their plans to protect Old Downtown. Portia wanted it noted for the record that she neither wanted nor valued anyone's opinion on the matter.

6. Natalie Buchanan moved to eliminate further Council talk from Society meetings. She was

outvoted.

I found Envy in her room painting her nails. She barely glanced up but motioned with her chin for me to have a seat on the edge of her bed. "I can't stop now or my nails won't dry right," she said. "But go ahead and tell me everything. I'm listening."

I told Envy what I'd figured out—how Fiona left the Crypt in the middle of the night to speak to Edgar. "According to Angelica, Fiona had a twisted sense of humor. She probably thought it was hilarious to scare Edgar's socks off while he was working. The corpses were never talking—it was Fiona the whole time."

Envy hrmmed thoughtfully. "Well, why was she reading meeting minutes? Seems a weird choice to me."

"Do you remember what Danielle said about how Fiona was willing to spy for Julian Gillespie's first mayoral campaign? I think she was doing the same thing in death—helping his campaign."

"Helping how?"

"I read over those minutes you found, and the Society talked a lot about city business behind the mayor's back," I explained. "They were even planning to run someone against him just so they could get access to City Hall's emergency shelter. I think Fiona was trying to warn him. She was a spy."

Envy scoffed. "So why not just *warn* him? Why read meeting—ohhhhh." Envy's face brightened as under-standing hit her. "She had that brain thing. She could only repeat things she'd read. She couldn't form her own sentences."

I grinned, glad my partner and I were finally on the same page. "Bingo. My guess is Fiona would have told the mayor directly if she could have, but according to Danielle, Julian's kind of a numskull. He might not have put two and two together like Edgar did."

"Do you think Edgar knew it was Fiona all along?"

"Probably not at first, but by the end, yeah," I said, smiling. "When people are that close for that long, they learn to recognize each other's quirks."

Envy tucked a lock of hair behind her ear. "So do you think Edgar warned the mayor in time? I mean, before he died?"

I leaned back, sinking my weight into my hands. Envy's mattress was soft—way too soft. I couldn't imagine sleeping on a bed like this. My back would be wrecked for weeks. "I don't know. According to Danielle, Edgar said he'd handled it. So I'd say he did. However…maybe we should tell the mayor what we know, just in case. Nothing we learned is earth-shattering, but politics should be done in public, not in underground, ghost-laden sanctuaries. If people from the city council are stabbing the mayor in the back, he deserves to know."

Envy blew on her nails while nodding. "I agree with you in theory, but man, haven't you ever heard of the Freemasons? Or the Illuminati? The whole world is governed from the shadows by rich people with an agenda."

"Now you sound like Wrath," I scolded, the slightest laugh rounding out my words. "When did you become a conspiracy theorist?"

"I'm not," she objected. "I just pay attention."

I chuckled. "Right. Anyway, Pam invited us to that Coldwater event, right? I guess the mayor will be there. We can try to talk to him then."

Envy glanced up and rolled her eyes. "Ugh, that fundraiser? Pride, I'd rather stab my eyes out with a fork than go to that. Why don't we just make an appointment to see Pam?"

"Well, Sloth already said she wanted to go, and we can't let her go alone. Plus, you're thinking about this all wrong," I pressed. "Imagine: you in a slinky dress, me in a debonair pantsuit." I didn't own a pantsuit, let alone a debonair one, but Envy didn't need to know that. "Us mingling with important people, Beefy Camera Guy there to film the whole thing? You have to think about your public image. It will look great on camera. Plus, who knows? Maybe there'll be celebrities there."

Envy only looked half-convinced, but I knew I was in. She would do anything for the 'Gram, plus, she really wanted to win this competition. Finally, she blew out a breath, her hair fluttering away from her face. "Fine. But as soon as I get bored, I'm leaving. And if there are no celebrities there? Then you owe me one. A nice dinner out or something."

I stood up and ran a hand through my hair. "So, how do you feel? It's fun to win an assignment, isn't it?"

Envy half-smiled and gave a shallow shrug. "I guess. But can I be honest? I really wanted to solve the Edgar Thornton case. Or the Chenoweth thing. Or find Charmaine. You know? I mean, I get it. We're just TV personalities. But I thought… I don't know. We were onto something big. Something *real*. And now I guess I feel kind of shallow."

I didn't want to say anything, but I knew exactly how Envy felt. She had just articulated how I'd been feeling ever since I had promised the detective I would stay out of his way. Figuring out how and why corpses were talking to Edgar Thornton was one thing. Figuring out who murdered the poor man was quite another.

"Keep the faith, Envy," I said. "Everything will happen exactly as it's supposed to."

I didn't know why I said that cockamamie nonsense. I didn't even believe that. As I turned to leave, I heard Envy mutter under her breath, "That's basically what I'm afraid of."

fifteen

. . .

We arrived at the Coldwater Mansion a little before 8 p.m. The gala was exactly what I promised Envy—rich people clad head to toe in glamorous outfits, carrying flutes of champagne and smiling prettily into flashing cameras. The event was a veritable Who's Who of Odyssey's cultural elite, and I couldn't help but feel a small swell of pride that my housemates and I had been invited. For her part, Envy looked to be on cloud nine. Her phone was glued to her hand, and she snapped pictures of everything that moved, making sure to use her front-facing camera as she posed for her audience.

Even Sloth looked genuinely happy for once. Envy had loaned her a dress, and her blonde hair was done up in a chic chignon. She actually cleaned up pretty well for a woman who spent her life cuddling people in stained pajamas. Even Beefy Camera Guy had dressed for the occasion, wearing a pair of tuxedo pants and a slim-fitting white t-shirt under a velvet smoking jacket.

We milled around the hors d'oeuvre tables piling our plates high with miniature quiches and tiny sausages until a voice drifted in from a nearby speaker. "Mayor Gillespie will begin his speech in exactly five minutes," the voice said. "We invite you into the main courtyard for the address."

I snatched up a second helping of tiny quiches as Envy groaned and downed the rest of her champagne. "You know, if we arrived fashionably late like I suggested, we wouldn't have to sit through the stupid speech." Envy caught the attention of a passing server and traded her empty flute for a fresh one. "Honestly, Pride. Your whole 'play-it-by-the-book' attitude is seriously cramping my style."

"Look at it this way, Envy," I said from around a mouthful of eggs and pastry. "If we arrived late, you wouldn't have so many photographs to post to your Instagram account."

That seemed to cheer her up, and the four of us piled into the main courtyard. I headed for the back row, but Sloth tugged me by the elbow to the front and shoved me down into the first empty seat. "You wanted to speak to the mayor," she reminded me as she slipped into the seat beside me. "What better way to snag his attention than to be right up front where he can't overlook you?"

Slowly, the folding chairs filled in as Odyssey's royalty and even a handful of ordinary citizens took their places. After a little while, the mayor strode onto the dais where he beamed his 1,000-watt smile at us. Pam was seated to his right, dressed smartly as ever in an elegant, crisp wool suit and pillbox hat. Small applause broke out around us, and the mayor placed his hands on either side of the podium and began to speak.

"First of all, I'd like to thank everyone for coming," the mayor said. "It's not every day I get a chance to address my city like this, and I cherish every moment we have together. I'd also like to thank the organizers—the volunteers and paid staff who put in so many hours to make the night possible. Can we give them a round of applause?"

Hoots and whistles broke out through the crowd, and even Envy clapped excitedly as she looked around. Sloth leaned toward me, whispering in my ear. "I love it when they thank the volunteers," Sloth said. "Putting on events like this actually takes so much effort. People don't realize it."

The mayor continued. "As most of you know, the purpose of tonight's fundraiser is to support a new expansion—the annexation of 200 square acres of land just outside city limits onto which we'd like to architect an important piece of Odyssey's future. Throughout our city's history, we've seen a lot of change. Odyssey used to be a small, undisturbed beach town, home to no more than 50,000 people. And long before that, it was a Catholic mission. Today, Odyssey is one of the fastest-growing cities in America."

Again, an enthusiastic group of applause met the mayor's words. I had a feeling he was stretching the truth more than a little. There was no way Odyssey was growing as fast as, say, Austin, Texas, or Boise, Idaho. It couldn't even if it wanted to—it was bordered by the

Pacific Ocean, so only so much development was even possible. Plus, while the likes of Portia Cameron and her cronies would love to see Odyssey become the next Beverly Hills, there were still families like the ghost Angelica that wanted to keep Odyssey's growth to a minimum and were working to make that happen.

So, he was pandering. Of course he was. None of people at the gala cared about Odyssey's gentrification problem. And the people who were most likely to be affected probably hadn't been invited to this shindig.

I squirmed in my seat. This kind of thing is why it's better not to have friends like Wrath whispering in your ear. Once you notice the man behind the curtain, the shine is totally off the penny.

Not that Wrath was my friend. But you know what I mean.

"As our city grows, we will experience growing pains. I have already asked the council for a plan to address our issue with the elementary schools, which don't have enough desks per classroom. I've also asked the council to put out an RFP for a developer—the high school football stadium is in dire need of an update. Go, Sirens!" He paused, presumably expecting applause, but the crowd was silent. No football fans among the social elite, apparently. The mayor collected himself quickly and plowed on. "For tonight, however, our focus is expanding the cultural arts in our beloved city. We will never compete with the likes of San Francisco, Los Angeles, or New York without a proper venue for opera, theater, or symphonies. So if you would, please reach deep into your pockets as you peruse the art on offer tonight. The auction will last until midnight, but there is a buy-out option on every piece."

I glanced over to see Envy fidgeting in her seat, tapping something I couldn't read on her phone. This was another reason we should have sat in the back. It was one thing to not pay attention when no one could see you. It was another thing entirely to not pay attention right in someone's face. I felt a hot flush of embarrassment crawl up my neck. I put a hand on Envy's knee and squeezed, but she made a disgusted sound and kicked my hand away.

"Before I let you all go tonight, there is one other thing I would like to address. As many of you know, we lost a good man recently. My good friend Edgar Thornton was taken from us much too soon. And though the police are doing their best to find the brute responsible, I fear Edgar's murder harkens to a deeper, uglier truth about Odyssey. And as mayor, I feel it is my job to bring light to the shadows and reveal the truth as I see it."

Now, I sat up a little straighter. Even Envy stopped typing, slipping her phone out of sight as she peered up at the mayor through the long false lashes she'd donned for the occasion. "Edgar and I spent many hours together alone in a fishing boat, sometimes speaking only a few words here and there for long stretches at a time. But the thing about friendship is, it weathers all things, including silence. Sometimes, no words are needed between friends. Yet at other times, it's your friends who illuminate a truth you've been too busy, too naive, or too unwilling to see."

On stage, Pam shifted in her seat, fingers skimming the necklace at her throat. Her eyes darted over the crowd. This obviously wasn't what the mayor was supposed to say, which of course made the spectacle that much more interesting. Usually, when politicians went off-script, it was a train wreck.

I leaned forward in anticipation. What can I say? I'm human; schadenfreude is my favorite pastime.

"Through Edgar, I learned of some disturbing goings-on here in Odyssey. It seems that a certain group of individuals—and they know who they are—have taken it upon themselves to form a secret society operating right beneath our fair city. These individuals masquerade as our friends and yet they stab us in the back. They pretend to have Odyssey's best interest at heart, and yet they plot the destruction of our friends and neighbors. But I'll have you know that as your trusted public servant, I will not take this affront lying down. Although the fire downtown has made it necessary for these grifters to temporarily relocate, I assure you that when they resurface, I will be there, ready and waiting, to grip their organization by the throat and squeeze until they are snuffed out. The underground of the city is like what's underground in people. Beneath the surface, it's boiling with monsters. But we will not allow *nefarious wickedness* to flourish here in Odyssey."

For a moment, the crowd was silent, unsure how to react. But little by little, people began politely clapping—more of a nervous trickle than actual applause. But something the mayor said grabbed me by the throat.

"Boiling with monsters," I repeated. "I've heard that before."

"It's something that horror movie director Guillermo del Toro said," Sloth replied. "I read it in an interview."

I blinked. "Huh. Well, I guess we wasted our time. He obviously already knows about the Paranormal Society and their plot to move their headquarters to City Hall. But maybe—"

"Shh!" Sloth hissed, her body going rigid. She gripped my thigh, fingers clamped down hard on the muscle. Her skin had gone stark white, her jaw clenched and her eyes open wide. I faltered, blinking in confusion. "Sloth? Are you—"

"The killer's here."

She said the words without emotion, and for a second, I thought I misheard. But then I saw the way her eyes darted around and she bit down on her lip. I sat ramrod straight. "What? Here? Are you sure?"

She nodded. "I head their thoughts when they mayor was speaking. I don't know who it was, but I heard it clear as day."

My heart began hammering against my ribs. "What did you hear?"

Sloth pressed her hands to her face. *"I guess I didn't have Edgar killed soon enough,"* Sloth said.

I opened my mouth in shock, but no words came out. Quickly, I pulled myself together and began scanning the crowd. I don't know what I hoped to see. It's not like I was gonna see the word *MURDERER* stamped across someone's forehead. But maybe someone looked nervous? Guilty? Ashamed?

But most everyone just looked confused and/or bored at the mayor's off-script ramble.

On stage, the mayor was finishing up his speech, gathering his papers and stepping down from the dais. Around us, the assembled crowd also began to disperse. I realized then that the clock was ticking. If we were going to find the killer, we needed to act fast, before people started leaving. I held my hands out before me. "What do we do?" I asked Sloth.

"There's only one thing we *can* do," she said. "And you're not gonna like it."

I braced myself. "What is it?"

My housemate took a deep breath. "You need to touch them, Pride. You need to touch everyone here and see if you have one of your visions."

I felt myself blanch. She was right—I didn't like that at all. If I'd learned anything about Odyssey, it was that almost everyone here had a secret, and I had no interest in seeing their dark thoughts.

But on the other hand, Sloth was right. I didn't see an alternative.

Envy grabbed me by the wrist and tugged me out into the center of the courtyard. "Just act natural," she said. "But move quickly, while everybody is still kinda bunched up. Like this."

Envy began winding through the crowd, placing a hand on the guests as she passed them—a touch on the shoulder here, a gentle brush against an elbow there. She smiled and purred as she weaved a path through the guests. She made it look effortless. But then again, she didn't have to worry about seeing anything awful or jarring.

Who knew what I might see?

But every moment I stood there deliberating was time wasted. So I took a deep breath, squared my shoulders, and followed Envy's lead.

I moved like a snake through the crowd, mumbling, "Excuse me," and "Beg pardon" as I slithered through the guests, touching them discreetly. The first person I touched showed me nothing. Nor did the second or third. The fourth person gave me a small jolt—an image of ashes falling from the sky and distant shouting. I shook it off as I moved past, making sure to casually bump into as many people as I could. But although I got flashes of memories here and there, I didn't see anyone thinking of Edgar's murder.

"This is hopeless," I said to my housemates under my breath as we moved into a cluster gathered near the art auction entrance. "I'm not seeing much. Nothing relevant, for sure. Sloth, do you hear anything else? Can you give me any clues?"

"I think it was a woman," she said, "but I'm not sure. The voice was hushed—angry. And the thought was quick—they immediately pushed it aside, like they knew better than to think about it. You know?"

I heaved a sigh and looked around. There were so many people; it would take all night to touch everyone, and I was already growing mentally exhausted. I was about to head toward another cluster of people when behind me, a familiar voice stopped me in my tracks. "Pride! I'm so glad to see that you all made it."

I turned around to see Pam standing behind me, hands clasped before her as she smiled brightly, head tilted slightly to the side. She was radiant as usual—whatever nervousness she'd experienced during the mayor's impromptu speech had clearly evaporated. She once again looked like the Head Woman in Charge. "Are you having a good time? Shall I fetch you a glass of champagne?"

I shook my head, stammering. Do you know how weird it is to go from looking for a murderer to being schmoozed by the city manager? It's enough to make your head spin.

"I've had my fill tonight, but thanks. It's a great party," I said, feigning a smile. "Though I have to admit, I do feel a little under-dressed."

Pam chuckled prettily and clucked her tongue against her teeth. "Clothes do not make the Sin," she admonished jokingly. "And anyway, your presence is more than enough. I don't know if you noticed, but some of our more celebrated guests have been eyeing you all night. Envy and Sloth, you too. The three of you don't seem to realize how popular you are. Have you mingled? Gotten to know anyone? Oh, speaking of that." Pam lifted a hand as her gaze shifted to someone standing behind me. She beckoned them over, and a moment later, a man was standing at Pam's side. He was dressed impeccably in a dark suit with a silver bowtie. He looked like he just stepped out from the pages of GQ magazine.

"This is my good friend, Travis Thornton. His husband Anthony is on the city council—Anthony's my right-hand man. I have to keep on his good side, since he knows where all the bodies are buried." She laughed and patted Travis's arm. "Travis, I'd like to introduce you to our town's newest citizens. Meet Pride, Envy, and Sloth."

I extended my hand, which Travis accepted graciously, his teeth flashing behind a handsome smile. "Wow, this is a real treat," he said. "I watch your show religiously. I can't believe I'm getting to meet you in person. Oh, *where* is Tony? I want him to meet you, too." He craned his neck, observing the crowd. "Oh, there he is." He wrapped his hands around his mouth and shouted. "Tony! Come here, babe, there's someone I want you to meet." Turning back to us, he scrunched his nose and said, "If he doesn't get excited, don't take it personal. He doesn't watch the show. I know. There's no accounting for taste."

A moment later, a man appeared from the crowd, sidling up next to Travis. When we saw each other, we both blinked in surprise, drawing up short.

"Tony Thornton," I said, offering my hand. "We meet again."

Tony smiled politely, accepting the handshake. "Nice to see you again, Pride. You clean up nice. I trust everyone is enjoying the evening? Pam, you look gorgeous as ever."

But even as he spoke, spewing compliments like a seasoned politician, I hardly heard a word of it. Because as soon as his fingers closed over mine, a scene flashed behind my eyes.

I was standing in a dark room, unfurnished but for a wall of metal shelves stuffed with cardboard boxes. Behind the boxes was a pegboard holding an assortment of tools—screwdrivers, hammers, a drill. Above, a bare light bulb hung from the rafters, doing little to illuminate the darkness.

And before me, gagged, blindfolded, bound with rope, and seated on a folding chair, was a woman.

I didn't recognize her at first. The blindfold covered most of her face, and her hair was tied back. She wasn't wearing any makeup, and her cheeks were wet and tear-stained. But then I noticed the way her nose twitched, and I thought I saw a glimmer of something that looked like whiskers.

It was Charmaine.

In my mind's eye, I was turning away, leaving Charmaine to whimper behind me. I was moving up the stairs, slamming the door behind me. And then I was in the living room. My eyes glanced over the walls, and I saw family portraits—a husband, another husband, and a young child.

I recognized the men in the portraits. One of them was pumping my hand even as this vision flashed through my mind.

Fleetingly, I saw a degree in mortuary science on the wall. I saw a pink backpack on the couch with the name *Rebecca* embroidered across the front.

I dropped Tony's hand and blinked, wiping my palm on my slacks to erase the memory from my mind. The vision hadn't lasted more than a few seconds, but it rattled me to my core. I was dizzy and light-headed, but I couldn't let on that anything was the matter. So I summoned my best reality TV smile and dredged up every ounce of charm at my disposal.

Turning to Travis, I said, "Say, I don't usually do this, but you wouldn't happen to have kids, would you? A little one at home who might like an autographed picture of an up-and-coming celebrity?"

As the words tumbled out of my mouth, I wanted to stuff them back in. Even Envy was looking at me like I'd lost my mind, and I couldn't blame her. It was easily the most cockamamie, asinine thing that had ever come out of my mouth, but I was operating on pure adrenaline and instinct. And the champagne I'd consumed wasn't helping, either.

But Travis's smile only brightened. "Our daughter Rebecca is eleven. She's asked to watch the show—apparently, all her friends are tuning in. I don't know if it's appropriate for children, though, what with Lust and everything. So I haven't let her watch with me. But she would be thrilled to have an autographed photo to show off for her classmates."

I stretched my lips in what I hoped was an approximation of a smile. "Why don't I have one sent to your house?" I said. "Here." I unlocked my phone and handed it to him. "Put your address in here, and I'll get that out to you. For Rebecca, you said?"

Travis typed and nodded. "Rebecca, that's right." He handed the phone back to me. "That's really generous of you. Thanks."

I glanced down, confirming the address. Then I slipped the phone into my pocket and gestured at Envy and Sloth. "Well, we don't want to keep you. I'll be sure to get that photograph in the mail. And I'll see if any of the other Sins want to include theirs, too. Anything for a fan, right?" I added with a wink. I glanced back to Tony. "Great seeing you again, really. Tell Danielle I said hi."

As we separated from the trio, Envy sidled up to me, clenching me by the elbow. "What was that all about? It's like you were channeling Greed or something. Where did you get that weird charisma from?"

I draped my arms around Sloth's and Envy's shoulders as I guided them hurriedly toward the exit. "I know where Charmaine is," I said. "I know who kidnapped her."

"Who?"

I gestured vaguely with a toss of my head. "Tony Thornton."

Envy gasped. "*No!* Danielle's brother? Edgar Thornton's son?"

"Charmaine is at his house," I said. "I saw it when I shook his hand. That's why I cooked up that signed photograph malarky. It got me his address."

Envy looked up at me, eyes blinking in what I think was admiration. "That was some pretty quick thinking," she breathed. Then she gestured to the camera guy. "We've got to get him back to Sinful House. We can't—"

"I'm not taking an Uber," the camera guy said. "Sorry. The Uber drivers in this town are—"

"No time to argue," I said, practically shoving my

housemates through the entrance and out onto the street. Beefy Camera Guy was right on our heels—he really would not be left behind. "We need to get over there now while Tony is distracted by the party. Let's just pray their kid went to the babysitter's house and not the other way around."

The four of us crowded into the car, and I pulled up Tony's address on the GPS. A moment later, we peeled out, hearts racing, praying we weren't too late.

sixteen

. . .

We parked a few blocks down from Tony and Travis's house. Thankfully, the street was dark, with few lights to give away our presence. By now, I was getting pretty good at breaking into places. It wasn't exactly the sort of thing I could put on a resume, but I'd be lying if I said it wasn't coming in handy.

The four of us sneaked around to the back of the house, looking for our way in. The back door was locked up tight. I could break a window if I had to, but that would make noise and possibly rouse the neighbors, inviting attention we didn't need.

"Let me see if I can find a key out front," Sloth whispered. "You guys wait here."

"You're not just gonna find a key lying on the patio," Envy whispered back. "Maybe we can use a hairpin to pick the lock."

"Oh, you never know," Sloth countered. "People find house keys on porches all the time on TV shows and movies. It must have a basis in reality."

Envy looked as dubious about that as I felt, but it was worth a shot. Beefy Camera Guy, Envy, and I waited while Sloth ran around the front of the house. From behind the house, we could just make out the sounds of pottery shifting around. A few moments later, Sloth appeared, a triumphant smile on her face as she brandished a key before her.

"It was hiding under a flowerpot, just like I predicted," she said, pressing the key into my palm. "See? All those shows I watch are really paying off."

I stared at the key in my hand, stunned someone was actually trusting enough to leave a key to their house on the porch where anybody could grab it. But I didn't have time to ponder the galactic stupidity of my fellow humans. I slipped the key into the lock and turned.

The door swung quietly open, and we all stepped inside, finding ourselves in the kitchen. Except for the illuminated clock on the microwave, the house was pitch black.

"Leave the lights out," I instructed. "We don't want to alert the neighbors that anybody's home. Let's use the flashlights on our phones and search for Charmaine. We have to be fast. There's no telling when they'll be back."

The four of us split up and began searching the house. I moved quickly from room to room, checking every corner for Charmaine's whereabouts. I wanted to shout her name to see if I could hear any scuffling or scraping or maybe some muffled sounds of her trying to alert me of her presence. But I was also worried about being overheard by the neighbors, so I kept my mouth shut.

Searching a house for a potential kidnap victim is more tedious than you might think.

I knew from my vision that Charmaine was in a basement somewhere. The trouble was, I didn't see any entrance to a basement. I checked every door I could find, but all I found were more rooms. I looked underneath rugs, checked baseboards for some telltale sign of a trap door beneath our feet. But I found nothing.

"I hate to say this," Sloth said, wiping her hands on her jeans as she joined me in the living room, "but I'm wondering if maybe you saw something else? Maybe the vision you saw wasn't in Tony's house?"

I pointed to a portrait on the wall. "I saw that in my vision," I said. "Tony definitely came up the stairs and landed in this room. There has to be a door to the basement in here somewhere. What am I missing?" I asked, mostly to myself.

"I don't know," Sloth said, peering around. "Maybe if we had a blueprint of the house, but…"

"That's it," I said, snapping my fingers. "Sloth, you're a genius." I said nothing more as I whipped out my phone from my pocket and dialed the only person I knew who might be able to help.

"Portia Cameron," the voice on the other end said.

"Portia, it's me, Pride. Listen. I need a huge favor. Do you deal with residential real estate at all?"

"Yes, of course. Though it isn't as lucrative as commercial."

"Do any of the residential homes in Odyssey have trapdoors? Hidden passageways? Stuff like that?"

Portia chuckled lightly. "Why? Are you thinking about making Odyssey your home permanently?"

"Portia, please. This is serious," I said.

"I'm being serious. And actually, yes, some do."

"How do you open them?"

Again, my question met with a pregnant pause. "Well, the mechanism differs from neighborhood to neighborhood. Different builders, you see. Bradley and Sons was the most sought-after builder during Prohibition, and they're infamous for—"

"Not now, Portia," I interrupted. "I don't have time to explain, but believe me when I say, this is a life or death situation. Are you familiar with the homes in this neighborhood? Uh, around 5508 Sundial Parkway?"

Portia was quiet for so long that for a moment, I wondered if I'd lost the connection. I looked down at my phone, but we were still connected. "Portia? Please. This is important."

Portia drew in a breath. "That's the Wateredge neighborhood," she said. "What are you doing there, Pride? Can you even afford real estate in that area?"

"Portia! For crying out loud!" I hadn't meant to shout, but this conversation was dragging on much too long. "I said this was life or death! Please!"

"All right!" She huffed loudly into the receiver. "Go into the living room. You should see a fireplace. Reach up behind the lintel until you find a button."

"What the heck is a lintel?" I screeched.

"It's the horizontal bar above the firebox. Just go feel around inside the fireplace along the top."

"That's it?" I asked. "Just press the button?"

"I can't guarantee what will happen when you press the button," Portia said. "Most people who have secret passageways and secret rooms in their houses go to great lengths to make sure the areas are secure so pets or kids don't get trapped inside. I can't tell you if they have installed a custom trigger or modified the solution another way." She was quiet only a moment before saying, "Pride, is everything okay? This conversation is troubling me."

I didn't have time to engage Portia in this line of conversation, so I disconnected and stuffed the phone into my pocket. I pointed toward the fireplace. "Portia says there's a secret button inside here."

I got down on my knees and reached up into the fireplace, feeling around in the dark. It was hard to discern what I was feeling. The bricks were very bumpy, and I couldn't really distinguish one brick from another. As far as I could tell, there was nothing in there except soot and dirt.

But just as my anxiety shot to astronomical levels, I found it. Something smooth, round, slightly protruding, and plastic-like. I almost missed it; it was smaller than I expected. With my breath held in my throat, I pressed the button.

For a moment, nothing happened. But then I heard a click, and the slightest movement caught my attention from the corner of my eye.

Sloth noticed it at the same time I did. "The bookcase," she breathed. "I think it just…"

She hurried over to the large wooden bookcase on

the other side of the room. Placing both her hands on its side, she gave a shove.

The bookshelf moved aside, revealing a staircase leading into darkness.

"This is just like an episode of *Scooby-Doo*," Beefy Camera Guy said. "Are you sure we should go down there? Maybe we should call the cops or something."

"Do what you want," I said, hands balled into fists at my sides. "I'm going in." I nudged Sloth aside, held my breath, and began my descent down the stairs.

At the bottom of the staircase was a light switch. I flipped it on, and a single, bare bulb hanging from the ceiling flickered to life.

The room was not so much a basement as a small cellar. It smelled of dirt and stone and something else I couldn't quite place. Musk? Body odor?

But then, of course it did. Because in the corner of the room, bound and gagged and perched awkwardly on the edge of a folding chair, was Charmaine Young.

Her eyes flew open in disbelief as she took in our ragtag group. As I strode over to her, she was trembling so hard, I thought I heard her bones rattling. But maybe that was the chair thudding against the floorboards.

Nope. On second thought, those were my teeth. I, too, was shaking like an unbalanced washing machine.

"It's okay, Charmaine," I said, going the extra mile to make my voice sound much calmer than I felt. My heart was thundering away in my ears, my monkey brain shouting out each second that went by like a sadistic countdown timer. "We're gonna get you outta here. It's okay." I said it as much for her benefit as mine.

I eased the gag from her mouth, and Charmaine heaved a haggard breath, licking and chewing on her lips. "How on earth did you find me? How did you even get down here? No, it doesn't matter, you can tell me later. Just please, get me out of here!"

Her hands were bound behind her back. The skin was raw and bruised where the bastard had tied her down. The knot was tight; I couldn't get it loose with my fingers. "Anybody got a knife?" I asked. "We're gonna need to cut her free."

"I'll get one from the kitchen," Envy said, darting up the stairs.

"How long have you been down here?" I asked, still working the knot with my fingers.

"I don't really know," Charmaine said. "Not long. I was at home reading lines for an audition when I heard someone in my house, and Anthony Thornton ambushed me."

A moment later, Envy placed a knife in my hands, and I cut through Charmaine's binds. She drew her hands to her chest, fingers rubbing the raw spots on her wrists. She would have some nasty bruises for a while— maybe even a scar. The rope had bitten into her skin pretty severely.

"Come on," I said, drawing Charmaine to her feet. "We need to get out of here."

"Oh, you're not going anywhere."

Charmaine froze mid-gasp as the rest of us spun around. My heart leaped into my chest as my eyes focused on the man coming down the steps, a gun in his hand.

A shadow fell across Tony's face as he glared at us from across the room. "Get your hands up," he barked. I threw my hands into the air—the others did the same. I felt Envy stumble next to me, her hands raised so high, she looked like she was about to do the wave at the local college football game.

"I see you found my selkie."

"Selkie?" Envy whispered. "What's a—"

"Shapeshifting seal," I answered. "He means Charmaine."

Tony snarled, his eyes darting from me to my companions and back again. "And here I paid good money for a home with a secret room. Seems I didn't exactly get my money's worth." He smacked his lips and offered a carefree shrug. "But it doesn't matter. I may not know how you got down here, but I know how you'll be leaving." The self-confident smile on his face widened, and he cocked his head to the side. "What is that they always say in the movies? The only way you're leaving here is in a body bag."

Under different circumstances, I might have thought it a very cheesy thing to say, and I would have made a smart quip about his lack of imagination or the quality of the movies he'd been consuming. (I mean, really, any time I hear mention of a body bag, I can't help but think about that scene from *Karate Kid*, and once someone makes you think of that flick, you just can't take them seriously anymore.)

But the truth was, in all the years of working for the San Diego Police Department, not once had anyone pulled a gun on me. It's one thing to have a clever remark at the tip of your tongue when the sun is shining, the wind is blowing through your hair, and the sand is shifting underneath your feet. It's quite another thing when you're staring down the barrel of a literal gun.

"You don't have to do this," Sloth said, her hands shaking in the air. "We don't want any trouble. We don't know anything about what's going on here. We just came for Charmaine. Just let us walk out of here, and nobody has to get hurt."

Tony sucked his teeth and dropped Sloth a sardonic wink. "We're long past that, though, aren't we? I mean, I just had to leave my husband alone at a party, and now you've invaded my house. I'd say this has gotten personal."

"You're a member of Chenoweth," I said, trying to keep the fear from my voice. "You're a bounty hunter."

Tony grimaced, something like disgust rolling over his features. "That's one way to look at it, I suppose. But I didn't join Chenoweth for the material rewards, though the prizes are pretty sweet. No, it was philosophical. Existential. Hunting supernaturals is just a means to an end."

"What's the end?" Envy asked. "What do you hope to gain?"

Tony gave a limp lift of his shoulders. "Status. Wisdom. Power. Why do people join the Freemasons or Skull and Bones or the Odyssey Paranormal Research Society? So we can grasp the numinous. So we can learn the secrets of the universe. There's great power in the world if you learn to harness it. Some of us understand that."

"Some of us?" Envy pressed on. "Who else? Walter Romanowsky?"

I threw a glance to Envy, ready to make my best "Now isn't the time for a Come-to-Jesus pow-wow with the crazy guy with a gun!" face at her. But when I saw the set of her jaw, I knew what she was doing. She was trying to force her muse ability to coerce Tony into talking. If we were lucky, he'd tell us something useful. But if we weren't…

"Walt? That moron?" Tony scoffed, disgust etched all over his face. "He never bought into our philosophy. He was just a greedy twit who wanted to watch Odyssey burn."

"Is that why he kidnapped Peyton?" Envy asked.

Tony gawped, taking a step forward. Instinctively, we all moved a step back. "*Walt?* Are you kidding? Walt didn't capture Peyton Cameron! That was me!"

The room fell silent, and Tony cursed, his arm shaking. "When I went to city-wide garage sale that day, I just expected to capture another supe," Tony continued. "I'd been tracking Peyton for a while. When you've been doing this as long as I have, you learn how to sniff out a shifter. The problem with Peyton was her high profile. She was Portia's twin. Capturing her at home or work was out of the question. But city-wide was my shot, and I took it." He grinned like a wolf. "I was 10,000 credits shy of a brand new Viking stove, and Peyton would put me over the top. But I wasn't ready for what happened when I snapped those bracelets on her wrists. I expected her to shift into a cuddly rabbit or a cute little kitten, but no! Peyton Cameron shifted into not one bird but *two!*

My future changed in an instant. To hell with a Viking stove—a shifter that could split was worth actual *money* to the right buyer. Good money."

Envy scoffed. "I thought you didn't join Chenoweth for the money."

"I didn't join for the money," he agreed. "But that doesn't mean I don't *need* money. It's expensive trying to keep up with the Joneses in Odyssey. I thought cryptocurrency was my ticket, but." He tsked and shrugged. "I was wrong. I lost a lot of cash, and that didn't go over great with Travis. Those birds were gonna save my marriage. So how do you think I felt when someone stole them right out from under me?"

No one said anything, of course. Envy's ability was working. All we had to do was let it run its course. The longer Tony talked, the more time I had to figure out a plan.

Except as far as plans went, my brain was coming up with zilch. Instead of hatching an escape, I just started praying for Gluttony's good luck mojo to kick in.

"It was my own fault," Tony continued. "I should have left the moment I captured her. But I set the cage down to browse a pile of vintage men's coats, and the next thing I knew…" He made a poofing motion with his free hand. "The birds were gone."

Now, I know I should have been wracking my brain for an escape route, but I was utterly transfixed by the notion of someone eschewing a profitable escape so they could explore the crummy wares at the city-wide garage sale. I'd been there before with Lust. And for the life of me, I didn't understand the appeal. The place was full of dusty old junk that should have gone into the trash heap. And yet this guy just confessed that he made the biggest score of his career and instead of running home to cash in, he was browsing old coats!

I'm telling you, some people just don't have the good sense God gave a woodpecker.

"I looked for those birds for months, but it was like they vanished into thin air. So you can imagine my surprise when I stumbled upon them at Walt's house a year after I'd lost them. His mother had them all along —and he was probably the one who stole them, that sleazy bastard. He must not have known what he had or else he would have sold them a long time ago."

"Walt's family is rich," Sloth said. "He didn't need the money."

"You know what people with money want more than anything?" Tony asked. "More money. No, my bet is he had no idea what he'd stolen from me. He was probably shopping for deals at city-wide like the rest of us when he saw the glow from the corner of his eyes. Stupid MagicBloc! I should have invested in a MagicThwart cage. Not as easy to get the supes into, but at least they don't glow."

I was too stunned to say anything. Were we really having a conversation about the pros and cons of different supernatural bounty hunting supplies?

"But birds are hard to offload if you don't know what you're doing," he went on. "The average supe collector doesn't want them. They're loud, and they don't cuddle. So I'm not surprised that doofus had trouble unloading them. But at least he took care of them. He'd acquired a bigger cage, and the birds looked healthy. So I confiscated them—after all, they were rightfully mine—and took them back to our lab at Chenoweth. After a few necessary experiments, I was *finally* going to capitalize on my find. But then you all burned the lab down and stole my birds. *Again.*" Noting the alarm on my face, he smirked. "Yes, everyone knows it was the idiots from *Sinful House* that caused the fire. Don't worry, though. I'm sure your network will take care of any impending charges."

For a moment, no one spoke. But then Charmaine's voice squeaked out, "Wait. Is Peyton alive?"

"You killed Eleanor Romanowsky," Sloth said, ignoring Charmaine. "You murdered an innocent old woman."

"Yeah, Wilson wasn't too happy about that either, actually," Tony admitted. "Fit of passion. It was never my intention to kill her. I just needed to make some money. And after losing the birds again, I still do. Do you know how infuriating it is to lose a windfall *twice?*" He turned his gaze to Charmaine. "A selkie isn't worth nearly what those birds were, but I never did get my Viking stove, so."

"Please, Anthony." Charmaine's voice was ragged, her words coming out a cross between a plea and a sob. "I swear, if you let me go, you will never see my face again. I'll leave Odyssey. I won't tell anyone anything. Just please, *please* let me go."

"I'm sorry, Charmaine. You're worth something alive, but your friends?" Our captor returned his gaze to me. "Not so much."

Tony raised the gun until the barrel was level with my chest. Then he fired.

…Or tried to. He pulled the trigger, but nothing happened. The world stood still for about a second before Tony realized he'd neglected to release the safety. He growled, thumbed the safety off, and aimed again.

But as his finger moved back to the trigger, someone hollered, an animal-like roar that filled my ears. I saw a blur of movement as Beefy Camera Guy plowed past me, throwing 260 pounds of pure protein shake-fueled muscle directly at Tony.

The momentum knocked the gunman to the ground. His hand crashed against the floor, and the weapon skittered from his fingers. Tony cried out with both surprise and pain as he tried to fight the cameraman off him. I was too stunned to do anything but stare. Thankfully, Sloth had the good sense to pick up the gun, her hands shaking so badly, she nearly dropped it.

"I don't know what to do with this!" she shrieked, unsure how to hold it or where to point it. The two men were still wrestling on the floor, and Envy and I were paralyzed with fear, neither of us able to utter a word. "Tell me what to do with this!"

"Drop it."

The sound of a new voice startled me out of my stupor. I turned, blinking with shock and confusion as another shadow descended down the steps. I knew that stance—the outstretched arms, the gun properly clasped in steady hands, finger off the trigger.

It wasn't another bad guy coming to escort us to our graves.

It was Detective Doyle.

"Nobody move," he said, coming fully into the room, his gun trained on no one in particular. "Drop the weapon, Sloth. Hands where I can see them. *Everyone! Now!*"

Sloth practically threw the gun down, her hands flying into the air. My shoulders were beginning to ache from holding my hands up, but I was so relieved to see the detective, I could have wept. My arms shook, but I raised them higher.

"Is everyone okay?" the detective asked as he turned toward the two men on the ground.

"I think so," I stammered. "You got here just in time. How did you—?"

"Portia called me," he said. "After she spoke to you, she called me, worried you were getting yourselves into trouble. Looks like she was right." He looked over to Charmaine and blinked. "Charmaine Young? Is that you? Are you all right?"

Charmaine pointed a shaking finger at Tony. "It was Anthony Thornton, officer," she croaked. "He's the one who kidnapped me."

Detective Doyle turned his gun on Tony. "Anthony Thornton, you're under arrest for the abduction and unlawful imprisonment of Charmaine Young. You have the right to remain silent. Anything you say…"

The detective moved in, angling the now-huffing and puffing camera guy out of the way and wrenching Tony's hands behind his back as he cuffed and Mirandized him. The rest of us watched in stark, disbelieving awe as the detective forced Tony to his feet.

"You'll save yourself a lot of grief if you tell me who else was in this with you," Detective Doyle said, guiding Tony toward the stairwell. "I know you're not the brains behind this. So who are you working for?"

"He murdered Eleanor," I called out. "He mentioned having an accomplice that day. He called him Wilson."

Doyle clapped Tony on the shoulder, barking out a dry laugh. "Let me guess, your city council buddy Wilson Brenner? Wow, the next issue of Stephanie Jones's newsletter is going to be a doozy!"

As the detective led Tony Thornton up the stairs, the sounds of sirens welled in my ears. The five of us stood in the basement in a near-circle, gazing at each other stupidly. Nobody knew what to say.

I turned to Beefy Camera Guy and licked my lips. "You saved my life," I said, my voice cracking with emotion. "You—I can't even—you really saved me." I bowed my head a little. "Thank you."

"Craig," he said. His eyes were steely, and his voice didn't tremble. "My name is Craig. So you can stop calling me Beefy Camera Guy behind my back." He looked down and gestured vaguely toward his midsection. "Anyway, this isn't all muscle. Some of it's fat. What? I like pizza as much as the next guy."

Moments later, the basement filled with uniformed officers. Someone wrapped a blubbering Charmaine in a fuzzy blanket and led her somewhere private to talk. The others took our statements.

I didn't know how long we were down there. But much later, when I was finally back at Sinful House and alone in my bedroom, I took off my shoes and lay down on my bed, eyes wide open. I was afraid to shut them. I was afraid I'd see that gun behind my eyelids.

I hadn't been lying there long when there was a knock at my door. I didn't answer, but the door creaked open, nonetheless. Sloth came in, padding quietly across the room until she reached my bed. She sat down and placed her hand on my shoulder.

"Pride," she said, "are you all right?"

I nodded mutely, unable to actually speak the lie aloud.

Sloth said nothing as she climbed over me, placing herself between my back and the wall. She slipped underneath the blanket and stretched her body along mine, and then draped an arm over my chest. At my back, she whispered, "It's okay if you need to cry, Pride. I'm a professional cuddler, remember? If you need to let loose, I'll take care of you."

Nothing happened for a few minutes. But slowly, a tear slid down my cheek. Sloth's fingers ruffled through my hair. I shuddered with the memories that came flooding back and squeezed my eyes shut. Sloth said nothing, didn't even move, as I quietly cried in her arms.

I must have cried myself to sleep, and when the ringing of my phone woke me the next morning, Sloth had already gone.

seventeen

. . .

I rubbed my eyes groggily and swung my legs over the side of the bed. I had half a mind to ignore the call, but when I saw the name on the screen, I blew out a hot breath and put the device against my ear.

"Charmaine, hey." My voice came out thick with morning phlegm, and I cleared my throat noisily. "Is everything okay?"

Charmaine was silent for a while. Then a small voice came over the receiver. "Pride? You weren't asleep, were you? I'm sorry to wake you. I…I just needed someone to talk to. I didn't sleep very well last night."

"No, I guess not," I said. "You've had a very traumatic experience. Are you okay?"

Charmaine chuckled darkly. "I'm not sure if I'll ever be okay again, if you want to know the truth. As long as I can avoid emotions for a while…" She snorted. "*That'll* really put a damper on my acting career."

I had to smile at that. If Charmaine was worried about her acting career after everything she'd been through, she wasn't as bad off as I'd feared. "I can recommend a therapist if you're interested," I said.

"Oh, I don't think that'll be necessary. Like I said, I just need someone to talk to." I was about to inform Charmaine that that was exactly what a therapist did when she pressed on. "I could really use some company. Would you mind coming over? I can make breakfast."

I couldn't imagine that Charmaine was worth much in the kitchen, but my stomach rumbled at the thought of breakfast anyway. I glanced down at the time. It was barely 9 o'clock, and I was usually not functional this early in the morning. But now that I was up, I *did* feel certain questions bubbling to the surface that only Charmaine could answer. "All right," I said, "breakfast sounds great. However… Can I ask you something?"

"I suppose so," she drawled.

I took in a breath. "What are you still doing in Odyssey?"

Charmaine was quiet for a long while. Then she said, "I'm not sure what you mean."

"Well, the police have Tony in custody, and I assume they'll nab Wilson for the break-in at Mrs. Romanowsky's soon enough. But…you and I both know someone else was behind all of this, Charmaine. And that someone is still at large. If they came after you once, they'll come after you again. Maybe not now—they're probably smart enough to wait until the dust settles. Still, staying in town seems dangerous. So, don't you think it's best to get out of Dodge? At least for a while?"

Charmaine sighed heavily. "Right. Well, that's very

practical advice, and I appreciate your concern. But I'm not going anywhere. This is my home."

I nodded. "All right. I'll be there over there in about 15 minutes."

"Wonderful. Oh, and Pride?" She paused. "Please come alone. The things I want to talk to you about don't need to be aired on television."

And then she hung up.

Fifteen minutes later, I was sitting on Charmaine's sofa, a plastic tray of croissants on the table before us and a fresh mug of coffee in my hands. For someone who had just been kidnapped, Charmaine looked remarkably calm and collected. Her hair hung in a loose ponytail at the back of her head, and she was draped in a fuzzy gray housecoat with matching slippers. She sat with her legs nestled underneath her as she leaned against the sofa's arm. "So." She took a long drink of her coffee before setting it on the table and clasping her hands in her lap. "How did you find me?" she asked.

"I got your address from Portia," I said.

Charmaine stared at me a second before barking out a laugh. "No, I mean, how did you find me at Tony's?"

I ran my hands through my hair and blew out a long sigh. "It's kind of a long story."

Charmaine tilted her head. "Tell me anyway."

I told her the whole thing, from finding Peyton to touching Tony at the party. When I was through, Charmaine bit down on her lower lip and nodded, her eyes welling with tears. "It's terrifying to be taken from your own home," she said. "At first, I thought he wanted to kill me. But then he was tugging me out the door, and I realized he was kidnapping me. That's when I tried to shift into my true form. Into a seal." Her cheeks blushing red at the confession. "I figured if I shifted, he'd never be able to haul me from the house. I'd be too heavy. But I couldn't shift, and I panicked. It wasn't until I was halfway out the door that I saw the can of Magic-Bloc fogger and understood. He was preventing me from shifting. I guess kidnapping a woman is easier than kidnapping a seal."

She wiped her face with the back of her hand and squared her shoulders. "Once he had me, though, he was so erratic. He kept going on about the trouble he'd be in if his husband or daughter found me. Of course, they didn't know about the secret room. He made sure to tell me that, too. To dash my hopes of discovery and rescue, I guess." She shook her head then, pressing her knuckles to a leaky nostril. "Honestly, I don't know how you live in a house for *years* and never know that you have an entire basement beneath you."

"According to Portia, some people pay good money for those homes. Presumably, those people have a lot to hide."

"Yes, I see that now," Charmaine agreed. "I did everything I could to get rescued. I screamed and banged on the walls, but then Tony tied me up and gagged me. He kept complaining that I wasn't supposed to be there in the first place. He wanted to move me somewhere else, but I guess that place burned down in the fire." She looked away, a far-off look in her eye. "That might be what saved my life."

I frowned. "What do you mean?"

"He didn't have a big enough cage for me," she said with a self-deprecating laugh. "If his headquarters or whatever hadn't burned down, he'd have a cage. And I'd be…" She shrugged. "God only knows where."

Halfway across the world was my bet, but it wouldn't do any good to say it aloud, so kept that to myself. "Charmaine, how did he even know about you? I mean, he was a bounty hunter, but he came for you very quickly after we rescued Peyton from the lab. Like he already *knew* about you."

Charmaine snorted and took a sip of coffee. "I was the worst kept secret in Odyssey," she explained, "thanks to that idiot Karen McMurtry. She just *couldn't* keep her mouth shut after she caught me in my natural form in my pool. I threatened to kill her if she told anyone, but I guess I'm not very convincing. Which more than one Hollywood casting agent has told me," she pointed out wryly. She sighed, shoulders sagging. "If it weren't for Walt, one of those Chenoweth idiots probably would have nabbed me long ago. But Walt used his family's money to keep me safe. To make sure no one laid a hand on me. But then he died, and his protection went up in smoke. I never even considered that until it was too late."

I fidgeted in my seat and took a sip of coffee to calm my nerves before settling back into the couch. "Charmaine…I have to ask. Why didn't you ever come forward with what you knew about Peyton's disappearance? Why didn't you tell anyone you'd been with her at the city-wide garage sale when she vanished?"

Charmaine squeezed her eyes shut and pinched the

bridge of her nose. "I've asked myself that many times," she began. "Why didn't I look for her harder? Why didn't I call Portia? Why didn't I come forward after I knew for sure she was missing?" The actress opened her eyes and blinked back tears. "And the truth is, I don't know. The Camerons are wealthy. I figured if Peyton was really missing, Portia would find her. Her money would find a way. Just like Walt's money kept me safe."

"What do you mean if Peyton was really missing?" I asked.

"Peyton and I were friends, but we weren't besties," she said. "When I couldn't find her at city-wide, I called her cell and left a message. I texted her. But when I didn't hear back from her…look, I know this sound suspicious in hindsight. But at the time, I figured she just went home. And when she *never* returned my call or my text, I assumed she'd hightailed it outta here, you know? Took a last-minute trip to Ibiza or wherever. Like I said, we weren't inner-circle friends. And by the time I realized she was actually *missing* missing…it was too late to come forward. I was scared I'd get in trouble. And plus, I didn't know anything anyway. So, what good could it have done?"

"It would have given the cops a lead," I said, incredulous. "That's how investigations work. You have to start somewhere! They could have found security footage. They could have interviewed vendors. They could have asked around if anyone saw her go in or come out. But you denied them that chance by withholding information. And as a result, you cost her a year of her life."

Charmaine slammed a hand to her thigh, her eyes

wild. "I know that! When I realized she was still alive, it was like a knife in my heart. I can't imagine being a caged bird for that much time. But I can't go back and undo what I did. And now, Portia will destroy me. I'm ruined in this town." She folded over, dropping her head into her lap, her shoulders shaking as she cried.

I let Charmaine cry for a while without offering her any comfort. For one, I wasn't sure whether she deserved sympathy. And for two, I don't like comforting people. It always made me feel like a phony.

After a few minutes, Charmaine finally calmed down. She took our plates and mugs into the kitchen, and when she returned, she looked almost normal. Her face was still red and splotchy, but at least she didn't have tears and snot running down her face anymore. She walked to the living room window and folded her arms over her chest as she looked out over the clear day. "May I ask one more question?" she asked. "Did you guys burn down their headquarters on purpose? Because the police are saying it was an accident."

I hadn't heard that, and the news made me smile. At least I wouldn't have to add *arsonist* to my resume. "Not exactly. Sort of."

Charmaine smirked. "Right. How did you find it?"

I considered lying, but I decided it wouldn't hurt anyone if I told her the truth. "I found a map inside Walt's laptop."

Charmaine turned to me, her face twisted in a confused frown. "A map?"

"A drawing of Old Downtown, with the old mission

marked with a star and a comment that just said 'Nexus of Power.'"

Charmaine was silent a moment, her lips opening into a small *o*. Then she coughed out a guffaw of disbelief. "He kept that after all these years? The map he got from that crazy psychic woman?"

Now, it was my turn to stare blankly. "What crazy psychic woman?"

Charmaine chuckled again, shaking her head as she tucked a stray hair behind her ears. "When we were teenagers, there was a woman who made a living pretending to see into the future. She'd dole out advice, and sometimes, she'd draw a picture of what she saw. And, of course, if she saw *darkness* around you, it only cost $100 for her to perform a ritual to cleanse your future." She rolled her eyes and huffed through her nose. "Anyway, Walt was enamored with her. He was really into stuff like that. One day, she drew a map of old Odyssey with that stupid phrase at the bottom. I'll never forget what she said when she gave him the drawing. She said, '*This place will be your beginning and your end.*'" Charmaine shrugged and continued looking out the window. "I can't believe he kept that piece of trash."

"It obviously wasn't trash," I said, frowning. "That paper led us to Chenoweth." I licked my lips, my pulse quickening as an idea blossomed in my brain. "Charmaine, tell me more about the psychic woman. What was her name? Does she still live in town?"

Charmaine leaned her head to the side as she thought. "Her name? Hmm, I'm not sure I recall. Daphne? Deborah? Something like that. Angelica

Muñoz was her daughter; she was in my graduating class. But they both passed away some time ago."

At the mention of the daughter's name, I sat up straight, my eyes shooting wide. "Angelica Muñoz? You're sure?"

Charmaine turned away from the window to meet my gaze. "Yeah, that was her daughter. Why? Does that name mean something to you?"

I bit down on the inside of my cheek, my excitement growing. "Yeah, it does. And you said her mother drew that map for Walt?"

Charmaine nodded, her brow knit in confusion. "Yes. Why? What are you thinking?"

I got to my feet, wiping my palms on my jeans as I stood. "I've got to go," I said. "I need to go talk to Angelica."

Charmaine held her hands out before her, beseeching. "I told you, she's dead."

I smiled. "Yeah, she is. See you later."

I left Charmaine bewildered by her window while I got in my car and drove once again for Déjà Brew.

eighteen

. . .

"**O**h, sure. My mom was a psychic. Everyone who grew up in Odyssey knows that."

I was sitting at a half-burned table with Angelica Muñoz in the Crypt. The other ghosts were giving us a wide berth, or at least appearing to do so. From the corner of my eye, I saw a few nosy specters lingering, their ears cocked in our direction. I surveyed the assemblage, looking for Eleanor. But I didn't see her anywhere.

"Was she the real deal?" I asked, returning my attention to Angelica with my arms folded across my chest. "I mean, I hope that doesn't come off as insensitive. But you know how it is. Some people will do anything for a buck."

Angelica sniffed, looking mildly affronted. "My mother didn't charge for services." Her face colored a bit, and she tittered, wobbling her head from side to side. "Well, at least not my classmates. She did that psychic stuff because she couldn't really help herself, you know?"

I huffed out a grunt of agreement. I knew. Being a psychic certainly had its ups and downs, but one of the downs is you can't always control who your gift is meant for. Sometimes, when I touch someone and I see something, I know deep down that I'm supposed to ask them about what I saw. Maybe offer comforting words or advice. I don't always want to. But if there's one thing I've learned about life, it doesn't really care one way or another what we want.

"Did she ever talk about the things she saw? Or was she more private about her gift?"

Angelica leaned her head to the side, murmuring to herself. "We talked about it sometimes. You have to understand, though, that my mother's psychic visions were personal. She didn't think it was right—you know, ethical—to share everything she saw. But sure, we talked about some things." Angelica leaned forward and tossed a stray lock of hair over a ghostly shoulder. "I have a feeling you're going somewhere with all of these questions, Pride. Call it paranormal intuition. Maybe you should stop being so cryptic and just get to the point."

I shifted, leaning my elbows onto the table between us. I wasn't sure why I was nervous about mentioning this to Angelica. It wasn't like what I had to say could put her in danger. She was already dead. Still, a chill ran down my spine. I had a feeling ears were listening that didn't need to hear what I had to say. But it wasn't like I could take Angelica somewhere else to have a more private conversation. Déjà Brew would have to do.

I gave a stiff nod. "Yeah, you're right. There is something specific I need to know. Do you remember that guy Walt Romanowsky?"

Angelica nodded. "Of course I do. Why?"

"Your mother had a vision about him. Apparently, he came to see her a lot. Does that ring a bell?"

Angelica shrugged. "I don't know how many times he came around, but I'm sure he did. He was kind of a weirdo. And my mother was kind of a weirdo, too. So I guess they sort of had an affinity for each other." She grew thoughtful then, her eyes narrowing as she peered into the surrounding darkness. "You know, he never came around here. I mean, as a ghost after he died. I never saw him here."

"Well, not everyone who dies ends up here," I said.

"No," she agreed. "But it seems like he should have."

I got that chilled feeling again, and I rubbed my arms absently. "Why?"

"I don't know," she admitted. "It's just a feeling."

The question of who became a ghost and went to Déjà Brew *was* a matter I wanted to investigate further, but now was not the time. "That doesn't matter," I said, waving this information away. "Your mother gave Walt a map one time. This is important. Do you remember anything about that?"

Angelica chewed her lips and shook her head slowly. "No," she drawled, "I don't think so."

"Think harder," I said. "It was a map of old Odyssey. And scribbled along the bottom were the words 'Nexus of Power.' Does that help?"

Now Angelica's eyes flew wide, and she snapped her fingers as memory struck her. "Oh! The Nexus of Power maps. Yes, I remember those. Well, I don't remember the maps themselves exactly. My mom was a psychic, but a great artist she was not."

Something Angelica just said snagged my attention. "Wait, *maps?* Plural? There was more than one?"

The ghost nodded excitedly. "Yes! See, some-times—rarely, but sometimes—my mother had visions that were shared between people. Like, she might have a vision about a cheating spouse or something. And of course, she would have the same vision for both the husband and the wife. Once in a while, she had a vision shared between people with no connection to each other. But with the map—she had the vision twice. The first time was for Walt. But the second time, she had the vision for someone else."

My heart stilled as my blood ran cold. "Do you remember who?"

Angelica's brow furrowed in thought as she made thinking noises in her throat. "I think so. Some woman? Walt was my age—that's why I remember his more clearly. I don't really remember all the old people that came in. I mean, you know, they weren't *old*, but I was a teenager, so."

Under ordinary circumstances, Angelica's rambling would have been annoying. But now, I found it absolutely insufferable. Still, she was doing me a favor, and I was the one who needed this information. So I took a breath to steady my growing anxiety and clenched my fists. "Angelica, please. Did she make a second map? Who for?"

Angelica tapped a finger against her chin thoughtfully. "Yeah, it was definitely a woman. Patricia? Penelope? Paula? Any of those names sound familiar?"

They didn't, but it wasn't like I knew every woman in Odyssey. We were getting nowhere, and with each passing second, I grew more anxious. "You don't remember the last name? This is really important," I repeated. I knew that reminding her of the importance wouldn't help jog her memory, but it was all I could do. I had to get her thinking and talking. I knew in my bones this information was crucial.

"Polly? Pepper?"

I froze. These were all P names. I breathed in deep and prepared myself for the worst. "Peyton?"

But the ghost shook her head. "No. Priscilla?"

My mouth went dry, making it difficult to swallow. My voice came out a squeak when I said, "Portia?"

As soon as I said this, though, Angelica snapped her fingers, and a wide smile spread over her face. "Pamela! That's it. Some lady named Pamela. She told both Walt and Pamela that this place of power would be their beginning and their end."

I breathed a sigh of relief. The last thing I needed was to find out Portia was behind everything I'd been through. "Okay, good. We're getting somewhere. What does it mean?"

Angelica sighed and shook her head. "I don't know. I'm sorry, but I guess that's a secret my mother took to the grave. I do remember one thing, though."

My emotions were already all over the place, so despite my better judgment, I went ahead and got my hopes up. "What?"

"Soon after Mom had that vision, someone bought Old Downtown. Almost exactly the property she'd drawn on that map, too. It was big news even back then —Odyssey has always gossiped about real estate. Mom was *so* annoyed about it. She said something like, if she'd known her vision would lead to such a large real estate transaction, she would have asked for a finder's fee." She winked at me, laughing at the memory. "So I guess you were right about my mom trying to make a buck. Just not in the way you thought."

I closed my eyes as I let these facts coalesce in my brain. Angelica's mother had a vision, and soon after, the property she'd envisioned got purchased. That couldn't be a coincidence. "Do you remember who bought the property?"

Angelica smirked. "Of course I do. Like I said, it was all anyone talked about. *What does a ventriloquist want with downtown real estate?* They said 'ventriloquist' like it was a dirty word, but that's how people get when they're jealous. Mean and petty. You should have heard the rumors. Some people even said—"

"Wait. Stop." I blinked hard, puzzle pieces slowly falling together in my brain. "Ventriloquist? Angelica, did *Fiona Arquette* buy this property?"

"You got it," Angelica said with a smile. "Though I'm not sure she was happy to end up down here. She kept muttering about monsters underground—she meant the Society, of course. She didn't like them much.

I can't say I blame her. They are kind of an odious bunch."

An odious bunch indeed. Some might even say —*nefarious*. I thought back to the mayor's speech about friendship, monsters underground, and nefarious wickedness. I thought of the Paranormal Society's meeting minutes, their discussions of city business, Fiona's alogia, and her friendship with both the mayor and Edgar. I thought of Pamela, the supernaturals, the Nexus of Power, and Chenoweth. I thought about underground tunnels and Spanish missions and the heart of Odyssey.

Two secret organizations had operated in the tunnels beneath Odyssey. Edgar had been talking about one. But it was the other that got him killed.

Suddenly, I understood everything.

A sick feeling welled in my stomach and suddenly, I was shaking like a leaf as I pushed back from the table. "Thanks, Angelica. I think I understand now. Oh man, I gotta get back to the house. I need to call the detective. I think I just figured out—"

The words were hardly out of my mouth when a voice behind me said, "Well, fancy meeting you here."

I cursed under my breath and turned slowly to see Pamela Arquette standing at the bottom of the stairs, a gun pointed at my chest.

You might think if you've already been through a scenario like this, it wouldn't scare you to pieces the second time. I'm here to tell you, you'd be wrong. "Hello, Pam," I managed.

"Hello, yourself. I've heard that criminals like to

return to the scene of their crimes. Still, it's quite a thing to see it with your own eyes." She offered me a tight-lipped smile, her head lilting genially to one side. "You burned down my laboratory, didn't you? No, don't lie, we both already know. Do an old woman a kindness. Tell me, how did you find it?"

I licked my lips. "Walt's map," I said. "The one I showed you when we first met."

Pam paused, bewildered, before bursting into laughter. "Are you serious? That terrible drawing was the map Devra made for Walter Romanowsky? *That's* what I sent Anthony and Wilson to retrieve? Oh, I wish I had known! I had no idea! My own map was carefully rendered. Not exactly a work of art, but not scribble, either. Oh, the irony!" She dabbed at her eyes and gave a rueful shake of her head. "That damn map. At least I had the good sense to destroy mine. I'd have destroyed his, too, if I'd managed to acquire it. But I guess you beat me to it. And now, here we are."

There we were, indeed. Surrounded by nothing but ghosts and the charred remains of the Crypt, I was keenly aware of how alone I was. Tonight, I didn't have Beefy Camera Guy to tackle my assailant. Detective Doyle was unlikely to come to my rescue. I'd managed to evade death once. Twice was asking for too much. But if I was going to die today, I would at least die with answers. "It was you all along, wasn't it?" I said, eyes trained on Pam's gun. "*You* killed Edgar. You killed him because you thought he knew about Chenoweth."

Pam blinked, surprised, but kept her gun aimed at my chest. She was doing that weird thing people sometimes do in movies, where she held the gun in her pocket and pointed her pocket at me. In the movies, the point is to prevent some random onlooker from seeing someone with a gun. Of course, that always struck me as odd for several reasons. The foremost is that if you see someone holding another person hostage with their pocket, you have to know there's a gun inside. But more importantly, we were alone in the Crypt. There was no one but us and the ghosts.

Pam heaved a sigh, her shoulders drooping in resignation. "Well, not *me*, but my men. It had to be done, you understand. I didn't want to kill him. Not at all."

"So why did you?"

"Sharing an office wall with Julian was usually only mildly annoying," she said. "Most of the time, I might hear him tapping noisily on his keyboard or laughing hysterically about something stupid he saw on social media. But occasionally, he'd stand in the danger zone, and I'd have to listen to every word of his conversation. The day before Edgar died—"

"You mean the day before you had him murdered," I cut in.

"—he rushed into Julian's office," she continued. "I couldn't hear everything—he wasn't standing in the danger zone for the entire conversation. But I heard him say something evil was lurking below the city. Monsters underground or something ridiculous. He said he'd uncovered something that could destroy Odyssey. That was the word he used. *Destroy*. He was so dramatic."

"You assumed Edgar meant to tell the mayor about Chenoweth," I said. "So you killed him."

"The mayor and I were headed to a meeting, and Julian told Edgar they would discuss the matter later. Edgar was adamant, but Julian sent him away." She tsked and rolled her free hand. "I knew at that point it was only a matter of time. You know what they say about the likelihood of a secret getting out. The probability equals the square of the number of people who know the secret."

I stared. While I was busy memorizing the quadratic formula to the tune of "Pop Goes the Weasel," apparently everyone else was learning this arcane but radically more useful piece of knowledge. My high school teachers had some explaining to do.

"I thought I got to Edgar before he told anyone what he knew. But you heard that little speech Julian gave at Coldwater. It seems Edgar got to Julian before I got to Edgar."

I sucked in a sharp breath and shook my head. "Edgar didn't tell the mayor about Chenoweth," I said. "He didn't know anything about it. Edgar was warning the mayor about the Paranormal Research Society!"

Hearing these words, Pam faltered, her eyes narrowing in the darkness. "That's ridiculous. The Society isn't dangerous," she spat. "They're just a bunch of layabout pretenders! Surely Edgar didn't think—"

"When Fiona died, your sister's ghost was pulled here to the Crypt, where the Society holds their meetings. She overheard them discussing city council business. So she went to Edgar and warned him that the Society was planning to run Portia against Julian next term. The Society operated here. *Underground.* Those were the monsters Edgar was talking about. It had nothing to do with you. You killed him for nothing."

Pam was silent for a long stretch. Then she said, "No, it wasn't for nothing. It was for Chenoweth and the important work we were doing here. I couldn't risk anyone finding the laboratory. Our work was groundbreaking. It was going to change everything."

I gaped at her, eyes wide in disbelief. "You were trafficking supernatural people for profit! How was that important work?"

Pam sucked her teeth and rolled her eyes but kept the gun trained right at my chest. "You think I joined Chenoweth for the money?"

"I think you—wait." Something she just said stopped me cold. "You *joined* Chenoweth? You didn't start it?"

Pam stared at me a moment before devolving into giggles, covering her mouth with her free hand. "Me? The founder of Chenoweth International? Goodness, no! You're giving me far too much credit. I started the Odyssey chapter, yes, but the whole organization? Of course not. We're worldwide. What, did you think I was manufacturing MagicBloc technology on my own? That I had warehouses of magical cat carriers and bird cages just down by the beach? That I was orchestrating the buying and selling of creatures during my lunch break? Really, Pride. I thought you were smarter than that."

To be honest, I thought I was smarter than that, too. Now that she'd said it all aloud, it was obvious she wasn't singlehandedly responsible for all Chenoweth was doing. The realization rendered me both disillusioned and petrified. Even if I got out of here alive and managed to turn Pam over to the cops, somewhere out there was an entire global organization hunting, capturing, and torturing supernaturals.

It was almost enough to push me over the edge.

But Pam was still talking, so I forced myself back into the moment. "Anyway, no, selling the creatures wasn't the point, but I did have to be rid of them once they served their purpose. The real work was in *studying* the creatures that Walt, Tony, and Wilson captured. How do they transform? What do they have that we don't? Can their essence be distilled, replicated, and absorbed by simple humans? That's what I want to know. *That* is my destiny!"

I cringed. People who tossed around words like *destiny* couldn't be taken seriously. When I was six, I thought it was my destiny to become the youngest member of the Harlem Globetrotters. But Pam still had a gun pointed at me, and I wasn't ready to join the ranks of the recently disembodied. So I gritted my teeth and asked, "Your destiny how?"

"It started with a map," she said, "and Devra Muñoz's vision. She told me this place was my beginning and my end. When I heard those words, I knew this property had to be mine. A 'nexus of power' right here in Odyssey? Tangled up in a psychic vision about *me?* I had to have it! But I made a mistake." A flash of sorrow crossed her face, and her nostrils flared. "I made the mistake of sharing that information with my sister."

Pam sighed, her eyes going soft and unfocused. "Like everyone, I adored Fiona. And I was so excited to tell her about Devra's vision. Even if she didn't believe in it, I thought she'd be happy that I found something special to pursue." She shrugged, and her expression edged toward anger. "How could I know Fiona was a double-crossing Judas who wanted me to fail? How could I know she secretly hated me for reasons I never really understood? How could I know my own sister would betray me?"

Understanding dawned on me like a baptism, and I heaved a slow sigh. "Fiona bought the property before you had the chance," I said. "Just to spite you."

"Not just," Pam said with an empty grin. "Also to *rent* me a place. To make me pay her each month for a basement room when the whole city block should have been mine. But she didn't even stop there. She recently decided to sell this place to a developer! Historic downtown! I told her I would buy it, but she refused me. Out of pure spite."

Growing up an only child, I'd always wished for a sibling, someone who got my sense of humor and shared my crooked nose. Someone I could blame for eating the cookies that mysteriously vanished from the jar. But after hearing Sloth and now Pam bemoan sisters who hated them for no reason, maybe fate had done me a solid.

But then I thought of Peyton and Portia snuggled together on the couch and thought, maybe not.

"At first," Pam went on, "I was devastated, then furious—at least until Anthony proposed we petition the city council to have this area preserved. Portia threw a wrench in that plan when she decided to run for office with her pro-development platform. But perhaps now that Peyton is home safe, she'll change her mind."

Pam's arm wobbled then, a subtle motion that quickened my heart. People don't realize how difficult holding a gun for long is. The body starts to ache. And Pam was already elderly; I wasn't sure how much longer she could hold out. As my hopes rose that maybe I'd get out of this intact, Angelica sidled up beside me, clearing her throat to gain my attention. "Pride? You realize—"

"Everything you've done is beyond unforgivable," I said to Pam, ignoring Angelica. "You kidnapped people. Experimented on them. *Sold* them. And then you murdered Edgar. And what did you learn, Pam? Did you even learn anything at all?"

The city manager scoffed, waving the gun in a circle. "We were close. I just needed more time. The answers are here, Pride! In this place of power! Everything that makes Odyssey unique, the reason wights and ghosts and shapeshifters are drawn here—it's all right here, under our feet, flowing through the earth. Don't you feel it? Don't any of you feel it?"

I opened my mouth to answer but then shut it again. I looked around—we were still alone. So, who was she talking to? I blinked, my brow wrinkling. "Any of *who*, Pam? Who are you talking to?"

"She's talking to *us*," Angelica said, her voice thick with exasperation. "Wow, are you ever dense. Haven't you figured out yet that she—"

"She can see ghosts?" I asked, incredulous. I hadn't forgotten about the gun, but my professional curiosity was eclipsing my human need for self-preservation.

Never let anyone tell you the human brain is logical. "Pam, can you see ghosts?"

Angelia threw up her hands in disgust. "She *is* a ghost, idiot! That's what I've been trying to—"

"I am *not* a ghost!" Pamela spat, swinging the gun toward Angelica. "Don't be foolish! I was attacked, but I got away! I was smarter, I was faster…I was…*better*…"

"You're *dead*," Angelica replied, her voice low and even. "I hate to break it to you. But you're dead. Finito. Dearly departed. El kick-o el bucket-o." She made a slicing motion across her neck with a finger, accompanied by a grotesque slurping with her mouth. "That's why you can see me. That's why you can see all of us." She gestured around at the ghosts lingering in the shadows. "Could you see ghosts yesterday? This morning, even?"

Pam swallowed, her hands quivering as she lowered the gun to her side. "No," she admitted. "But that doesn't mean…it can't mean…"

"Lots of these folks didn't realize they were dead at first, either," Angelica said, gesturing at the surrounding ghosts. "I don't know how. When I died, I saw my body. I knew what was up. But anyway, it's not unusual."

My phone rang then, and I dug it from my pocket, pressing the shattered screen to my ear. "Look, now's not a great time," I said.

"Pride, where are you?" The voice on the other end belonged to Envy, but she sounded strained. "You need to come home. There's been a development."

"Development?" I glanced over to Pam, who was no longer paying attention to me. She walked to an empty armchair and sank down into it. "What development, Envy?"

"It's the mayor," she said. "He's been arrested."

I blinked in surprise. "Arrested? Wait, why? What for?"

Envy was silent for a moment. Then she said, "For the murder of Pamela Arquette."

I let that sink in as I looked over at Pam. She was watching me intently with an expression I couldn't read. Now that I knew, I couldn't believe I'd missed it before. She shimmered slightly, and she had a dark bruise at the base of her throat. Maybe a crushed windpipe? I tried not to think about it. "Okay," I answered. "I'm on my way." I ended the call and slipped the phone back into my pocket. "You don't have a gun at all," I said to Pam. "You tricked me. You're a ghost—you can't hold a gun."

Pamela smiled sadly and removed her hand from her pocket. She was making a finger gun with her thumb and forefinger. "I've never owned a gun," she admitted, "but I've seen enough movies to know you don't need a gun to hold someone at gunpoint. You just need a pocket and conviction. Oh, I wasn't sure you'd fall for it," she admitted. "But it was worth a shot. And look at us! It worked! I guess fear does funny things to people."

"What were you going to do with a fake gun?" I asked, bewildered. "What was your plan?"

She patted her hair and leaned her head to the side. "Old Downtown may have burned up, but these tunnels are hardy. Surely there's a cage or two left at the lab. I was just going to lock you up and throw away the key if you want to know the truth."

She smiled then, and a shiver ran down my spine. She was so calm and cool, like locking another person in a cage meant nothing to her. But I guess if you'd done it once, you could do it again. Except, I didn't think she *could* do it again because she was a ghost. But apparently, she didn't know that. "How did you even know you'd find me here? And how did you know I was onto you?"

"Oh, I didn't," she said. "I didn't plan to come here at all. I was just…pulled. Same as Fiona, I guess."

I glanced over at Angelica, who was nodding with understanding. She, too, had been pulled to the Crypt after death.

"But when I saw you," Pam continued, "I hatched a plan. My supernaturals may be gone, but a ghost-whispering psychic wasn't a bad alternative for study. Especially one who was also the sole survivor of the Sam Lovelace commune." She laughed then, a dry, mirthless sound. "So no, I didn't know you were onto me. Not until you accused me."

"You're a sick, evil woman. But I guess now you're a sick, evil corpse. Murdered by your own colleague. The mayor."

The smug expression slipped from her face, and her eyes glazed over. "The mayor," she repeated, nodding softly to herself. "That's right. He attacked me in my own home. Yes, I remember now. He came to my home to tell me the police connected Charmaine's kidnapping and Edgar's murder thanks to the foggers Anthony left behind. Idiot. He named me, of course. After everything I did for him. Getting him on the council, getting him into Chenoweth…Well, I should have known better. If you want something done right…"

She shrugged, a wan smile playing over her lips. "Julian may have been a dolt, but he did one thing right. At least he had the guts to avenge his best friend's murder himself."

"Pamela," I said, my throat going dry, "did you say *Tony* left the fogger behind at Remembrance Home? Does that mean Tony killed his own father? Just because you asked him to?"

Pam smirked and looked away. "I told you," she said. "Family isn't all it's cracked up to be."

I turned to Angelica. "I have to go," I said. "Is it okay to leave her here with you? She's a murderer," I reminded her. "You don't deserve to be burdened with her, but I don't know what else to do."

"Don't worry about me," Angelica said. "Go home and get some rest. You've earned it."

———

When I arrived back at Sinful House, Envy was waiting for me on the stoop. Without a word, she ran up to me and threw her arms around me, pulling me close.

And the crazy part was, I let her.

When we disentangled, I said, "I saw Pam. It's a long story, and I'll tell you everything later, after I've processed it. But the short version is, Pam was behind the Chenoweth chapter in Odyssey. With her and Walt gone and Tony and Wilson behind bars, the supernaturals in this town are safe."

Envy looked up into my face, her eyes shining. "That's great, Pride. That's…wow." She smiled, shaking her head. "This day is really coming around."

I lifted an eyebrow. "What do you mean?"

"Well, I have some good news of my own." Envy smiled and ran a hand through her hair. "I think all this is over. Whatever we were supposed to do or learn…I think we did it."

I frowned. "What are you talking about?"

Envy gestured to the surrounding yard. "See for yourself. Notice anything?"

I stepped away from Envy and looked around. "Not really," I began. "What—"

But then I saw what Envy meant. Or rather, I *didn't* see.

The Star of the Sea, that mysterious harbinger of tragedy and misfortune, was gone.

nineteen

. . .

"So Fiona was behind the talking corpses the whole time?"

Envy and I were sitting with Danielle Martin and her husband Hank at Remembrance Home. My housemate and I had taken the two armchairs, and the Martins were ensconced on the couch. Beefy Camera Guy—no, *Craig*—was on his feet, filming from the wings.

"That's right," I said. "Thanks to her alogia, she couldn't relay the information she discovered in her own words. The best she could do was recite the meeting notes to your father. But to his credit, he was smart enough to figure out the significance of what she said. And then he told what he knew to Julian."

Danielle's lips pinched, and her face blanched a little. "That information got my father killed," she said, her voice breaking. "And my own brother pulled the trigger."

My face burned hot at that, and I dropped my gaze.

When we'd first begun this investigation, Envy and I both knew the police would target Tony Thornton as their number one suspect. We were sure that was wrong, and that's why we'd gotten involved in the first place. Of course, that was right, just for all the wrong reasons. He hadn't killed his father to quickly inherit the business and get out of debt. He'd killed his father because he was fanatically committed to an organization that had no respect for the value of human life.

I couldn't imagine how difficult it must have been for Detective Doyle to tell Danielle that her brother murdered her father. Looking at her now, I saw the despair all over her face. In a matter of days, she'd lost her father and her brother. It was heart wrenching.

"He used the MagicBloc fogger to douse the preparation room. He wanted to make sure your father never told anyone what happened. Talking corpses, after all," Envy explained. She folded her hands in her lap. "I'm so sorry to tell you all this."

Hank reached for his wife's hand and gave it a little squeeze. "Hopefully, Tony will get the rehabilitation he needs in prison. And now your father is in a better place."

I leaned forward, my fingers steepled beneath my chin. "Well, actually—"

Envy cleared her throat, and when I glanced at her, she tucked a lock of hair behind an ear and gave her head a little shake. It was a subtle enough gesture, but I deciphered it well enough. *Shut it, Pride*, she was saying.

I shut it.

"I'm really thankful for everything you discovered,"

Danielle said, oblivious to my little exchange with Envy. "I knew I could count on you." A soft but sad smile spread over Danielle's face. "I hope I never *need* your services again, but if I ever do, can I call you directly?"

I drew my eyebrows together in confusion. "Call us directly? You mean…like your own personal investigation team or something?"

Danielle tittered, her cheeks blooming pink. "Well, when you say it like that, it sounds ridiculous. I guess that's not what I meant, anyway. I just meant…I don't know, as a friend?"

In all the years I'd been helping people find the culprits behind their loved one's deaths, no one had ever asked if I would be their friend. I was so choked up for a moment that I hardly knew what to say. I looked at Envy, hoping she knew how to fill the silence. It seemed the situation was so strange that even her muse magic wasn't working on me.

Thankfully, my housemate clapped her hands together and giggled happily. "Of course! We should all get together and have lunch sometime. I hear Jorge's on the Coast has great seafood and beautiful dinnerware— we could take *great* photos for Instagram!"

Danielle laughed as she nodded, the last of her grief melting away. "Wonderful. I'd really like that."

The four of us stood, and the Martins led us outside. Hank walked us to our car while Danielle stayed behind on the porch, waving on her tiptoes.

"Drive safe," he said, shutting the driver's door as I buckled in.

As Envy fiddled with her seatbelt, I turned on the

radio, cranking up the volume louder than usual. I felt a weird sensation forming in my chest, just behind my rib cage. It felt warm, like I was developing a fever. It also tickled, like I was about to develop a cough or a sore throat. But I didn't feel fatigued or run down.

And then I found myself smiling like an idiot and even jamming to the music a little. Because I realized I wasn't getting sick. I was just really happy.

Days later, it was time for our inevitable house gathering with Tricia Woodward to hear our weekly results. Usually, Gluttony whipped up something delectable for the event, but today, he'd sent me out for treats. I carried a pink box filled with pastries from Bake Some Waves into the kitchen and plopped them down next to a stack of paper plates.

"Honey, I'm home!" I shouted. I selected a pastry for myself and headed into the rec room where the rest of the cast and our producer was already waiting. Tricia was dressed in a heather gray t-shirt dress and a pair of white canvas tennis shoes. Her hair was pulled into a messy bun atop her head, and a simple pair of pearl earrings studded her earlobes. She looked picture-perfect as usual.

As I entered, she looked down at her watch and tsked. "You're late," she admonished. "We've been waiting for fifteen minutes. Where are the snacks?"

"Kitchen," I said, jamming a thumb over my shoulder. "Do you want me to bring you a plate?"

Tricia scrunched up her nose and gave a disdainful shake of her head. "I haven't eaten carbs since the 90s," she said. "Well! Now that we have everyone, let's get started."

I wedged myself on the couch between Sloth and Gluttony. "I didn't know we were on a schedule," I muttered, taking a bite of lemon bar. The ooey gooey sweetness melted on my tongue. The tartness made my toes curl. "Did you know we were on a schedule?"

"I bet you're all dying to know how you did this week," Tricia was saying. She was standing at the front of the room, shining her 1000-watt smile around the room. "But before I read the results, I want to remind you that the viewers haven't seen any of your footage from your most recent challenge. These are the results from the episode which just aired tonight."

"We know that, Tricia," Gluttony said. "You tell us the same damn thing every week. We ain't dumb. Just get on with the numbers." To me, he said, "Yes, of course I knew. That's why I sent you to get the snacks. I didn't have time to cook nothing."

"You could've given me a heads up," I whispered. "Should I bring the pastries in here?" I turned to Sloth. "You won't make a mess, will you?"

"I also want to remind you," Tricia continued, unruffled by the interruption, "that these numbers are not cumulative. These are only today's results. So! Drumroll, please!" She brought out her phone and peered down into the screen. "Without further ado, tonight's results are as follows!

"In seventh place with 7% of the vote is Greed."

Tricia pulled a face of mock sorrow and sucked her teeth. "Ooh, better luck next time, buddy. Pride, you came in sixth place with 10%." She clucked her tongue against the roof of her mouth. "I guess you should have gone to Santa Barbara to check out that art piece like we talked about."

My jaw dropped. Tricia was still talking about Santa Barbara and finding clues about that stupid missing commune? Did she not realize I'd just been involved in a case where two people were murdered, one was kidnapped, and an elemental on a rampage burned an entire city block to the ground?

And she was coming at me about *artwork?*

"I guess I was busy," I muttered, not wanting to appear too flustered. The truth was that 10% was a blow to my ego. Nobody likes to lose, but that was just *harsh*.

"In the future, when I give you advice, you should take it," Tricia said with a breezy shrug.

"Wait, hold on." Wrath was on his feet now, hands planted on his hips. "You've been giving audience-winning tips to Pride? What about the rest of us?" He gestured wildly at the other housemates. "What are we to you, chopped liver? Or are we just not as valuable for your precious capitalist ratings?"

"Pipe down, Wrath," Lust said from her seat. "Tricia gave me some tips, too. Why do you think I've started wearing more red? Red pops on camera."

"I don't notice what you do or don't wear," Wrath said, rolling his eyes.

Lust blinked in mock surprise. "You don't?" As she

said this, she tugged down the front of her blouse just a little.

Wrath blushed and sat down, arms folded over his chest. "All I'm saying is, I want a fair shot. That's all."

"You won last week," Tricia reminded him. "So I think you're doing just fine."

Sloth must have noticed my despondency because she leaned into me, throwing her arm around my neck. "Don't listen to Tricia," she said. "She's the producer. She gets paid to bring drama to the house. For what it's worth, I think you made the right decision to put off going to Santa Barbara. Your task was a whopper." She grinned, showing charmingly crooked teeth. "Anyway, just my two cents. But I know my opinion doesn't really count."

"It counts," I said, offering her a genuine smile. The more time I spent with Sloth, the more I liked her. Even if she did leave crumbs and smears of jelly everywhere she went. "Thanks."

"No problem. So, do you think your old girlfriend watches the show? And if so, do you think she votes for you?"

My hands turned to ice, and I stammered, rubbing the nape of my neck as a hot flush crawled into my face. "I have no idea," I said. "Probably not? She doesn't watch much television."

Sloth twisted her mouth in thought. "Well, my family doesn't watch that much TV, either. But they watch *Sinful House* because I'm on it. So maybe your girl-friend is watching, too."

"She's not my girlfriend anymore," I answered automatically. As soon as the words were out of my mouth, I lifted my gaze to find Lust watching me from across the room, a coy smile on her lips.

I blushed even harder and looked away.

"What's going on there?" Sloth asked, her eyes flitting toward Lust. "I noticed you've been avoiding her."

I huffed and chewed my lips. "Nothing's going on there," I said. "I just…I don't know, maybe dating someone at the house isn't the right move. This is work, you know? Better to keep business and personal separate."

Sloth hrmmed and twirled a pigtail around a finger. "Maybe," she drawled. "But maybe not. Whatever you decide, you should make it clear to her. For both your sakes." She ruffled my hair with her fingers and winked.

I chanced another glance at Lust and saw she was going out of her way not to look at me. I wasn't sure what that meant, but Sloth was probably right. The tension between us needed to be addressed one way or another.

Just maybe not tonight.

"…everything for next week," Tricia was saying, apparently wrapping up her announcements. "For now, please congratulate Sloth and Envy on this week's tie! Well done!"

Tricia was already heading over to offer Sloth a congratulatory hug before I had processed what I'd just heard. I turned to my housemate and smiled. "You won?"

"First time for everything!" she beamed. "Mom and

Dad will be thrilled! Take that, Hadley!" she said, making a rude gesture in her sister's honor.

She sank back into the sofa and pulled out her phone. "So, should we check our next assignment?" she asked.

I blinked and ran a hand over my hair. "Our assignment? We're on the same team?"

Sloth laughed and nudged me in the side with her elbow. "Wow, you really weren't listening to Tricia at all, were you?"

"No," I admitted. "I was talking to you."

Sloth chuckled and wriggled back into the cushions. "I guess that's fair. Most people can only really pay attention to one conversation at a time. I have an advantage." She tapped her temple with a forefinger. "Tricia's a loud thinker. I plucked my teammate right out of her skull."

On my other side, Gluttony cleared his voice. "It's us three this week," he said. "And with our combined talents, I think we have a really good shot."

"We do," I agreed. "You know, I've been meaning to thank you and just haven't had the chance."

Gluttony grunted. "You're welcome. What for?"

"For the good luck popcorn," I said. "You were right. The whole house was acting like we were doomed, and we really needed that little pick me up. And for what it's worth, it really came in handy. I think it saved my life. Twice."

A slow, embarrassed grin spread over Gluttony's face. "Ayo, if something saved your life, it wasn't my good luck magic."

I blinked. "What do you mean?"

"I mean I ain't never put no good luck magic in that popcorn. I just said I did because y'all was acting like you'd been condemned. Look, far as I know? Ain't no such thing as good luck or bad luck. It's all in your mind," he said, tapping his temple for emphasis. "Things happen. There's nothing either good or bad. It's *thinking* that makes it so."

"*Hamlet*," Sloth said with a smile. "My favorite Shakespearean play. And you're right," she added thoughtfully. "There's no fate but what we make."

"*Terminator!* Nice one." Gluttony and Sloth high-fived each other right over my head. "Should we read our assignment?"

"Hold on," I said. "No fate but what we make? Then how do you explain Greed's premonition? He predicted Envy would summon a fire elemental that put us in danger, and she did!"

"Or," Gluttony drawled, "she did *because* Greed put the idea in her head. If he had never said anything, would she still have summoned it?"

"What's really going to bake your noodle later on," Sloth intoned, "is would you still have broken it if I hadn't said anything?"

"*The Matrix!* Dang, girl. That's good." Gluttony pointed at Sloth with admiration.

"Reality is shaped by your beliefs," Sloth said with a definitive nod. "That's why I try to keep my thoughts clean and positive. And also why I watch a lot of sci fi."

I was still grappling with the realization that Gluttony had lied to me and that magic hadn't saved me at all. The fact that I wasn't dead was just pure, dumb…

…well, luck.

But I didn't have the chance to dwell on any of that because Sloth opened up her email and leaned over me so all three of us could get a good look at the screen. "Ready?" she asked.

"Let's get it," Gluttony said.

Sloth navigated to the email with the subject line, "Sloth, Pride, Gluttony Task #4," and clicked it.

It read:

"Local fashion designer Julio Villarreal has opened a new boutique attracting huge crowds from all over southern California—but for the wrong reason. The Star of the Sea appeared at his doorstep, and gobs of tourists are camped out at the site of the miracle. Julio says it's ruining his small business. Your task is to discover the Star of the Sea's mysterious secret and put her back in her rightful place once and for all."

"More statue nonsense," Gluttony grumbled. "I thought we was *done* with homegirl."

I looked up to see Tricia ambling toward us, arms folded nonchalantly over her chest. "Everybody good here?"

"Just looking over our assignment," I said. "This one hits close to home."

"Portia Cameron specially requested you for this task," Tricia beamed. "She said putting the statue to rest would help with her campaign. She's running on an anti-supernatural, pro-business platform."

I blinked. "Really? She's still running? I assumed

after finding her sister, she'd change her mind about running for mayor."

"Well, someone has to," Tricia pointed out. "According to Odyssey's laws, in the event the mayor becomes unable to perform his duties, an emergency election must be held. And since Pam Arquette was the city manager, well, it means Odyssey is hurting for leadership right about now."

I snorted. "Well, she can't be serious. How can she run on an anti-supe platform when her own sister is a supernatural?"

"People act against their own best interest all the time," Sloth said with a knowing nod. "We're complex creatures, Pride. You, me. Even Portia."

I gave an unconvinced grunt. Sure, maybe that was true. But if I knew Portia, there was more going on with her than met the eye. Her interest in the statue wasn't just about winning an election. She wanted to uncover the mystery of what made Odyssey…well, Odyssey.

And though I hated to admit it, so did I.

"I guess that's true," I conceded, sticking the last of the pastry in my mouth. "Well, with any luck, no one will turn up dead this time."

The producer shrugged and offered a mysterious smile. "Well, don't speak too soon. Stranger things have happened in this town. And just think of the ratings!"

I didn't like the sound of that, but I didn't have a chance to dwell on Tricia's ominous message for long. As the producer walked away, Sloth slipped her phone into her pocket and looped her arm over my shoulders. "One thing about Sinful House," she said, "this place is never boring. I guess that's why we're still on the air. Right, Gluttony?"

"That's right," he agreed. "And we about to keep it that way. I hope that mermaid is full up on sightseeing because her traveling days are numbered."

I blew out a hot breath and swallowed down the last of my lemon bar. I had no idea how to catch a wandering mermaid, but if there was one thing I'd learned in my time at the house, it was that Odyssey, California was full of surprises.

thanks for reading!

Sinful House Mysteries was so much fun to write, and I'm thrilled to share these adventures with you.

I'd love it if we kept in touch.

If you'd like that too, please sign up for my newsletter on my website.

If a newsletter isn't your jam but you'd still like to support me, please consider leaving a review. This is the easiest and best way to help other readers connect with the weird and wonderful cast at *Sinful House*.

See you soon!

about the author

Amber Fisher is the author of urban fantasy and paranormal mysteries ranging from sweet and delightful to dark and morbid. She lives in Austin, Texas, where she enjoys watching sci-fi shows, making things with her hands, baking, and playing tabletop games with her husband.

Connect with me at: amberfishermedia.com

Facebook at: facebook.com/amberfisherauthor

Twitter: @amberla

Sign up for the newsletter: bit.ly/332eurl